Later, much later, w

We heard a little sawing, singing sound as a file began to slice through screen wire. From the settee Mary Alice made some tiny, terrified sound. Grandma reached down for something in her sewing basket. The darkness made me see pinwheels like sparklers. I just managed to notice Grandma's rocker was rocking and she wasn't in it. She was standing over me. "Keep just behind me," she whispered.

I followed her across the room to the kitchen. You wouldn't believe a woman that heavy could be so light on her feet. She floated, and we moved like some strange beast, big in front, small behind. Now we were by the door to the kitchen, and I heard the scuffle of heavy feet in there on the crinkly linoleum. . . .

＝ঌৣৎ＝

★ "Part vaudeville act, part laconic tall tale, the stories, with their dirty tricks and cunning plots, make you laugh out loud at the farce and snicker at the reversals. Like Grandma, the characters are larger-than-life funny, yet Peck is neither condescending nor picturesque. . . . Many readers will recognize the irreverent, contrary voices of their own family legends across generations." —*Booklist*, starred review

★ "Each tale is a small masterpiece of storytelling."
—*The Horn Book*, starred review

A NEWBERY HONOR BOOK

PUFFIN MODERN CLASSICS

Richard Peck

A Long Way from Chicago

A NOVEL IN STORIES

PUFFIN BOOKS

PUFFIN BOOKS

Published by Penguin Group

Penguin Young Readers Group,

345 Hudson Street, New York, New York 10014, U.S.A.

Penguin Books Ltd, 80 Strand, London WC2R ORL, England

Penguin Books Australia Ltd, 250 Camberwell Road, Camberwell, Victoria 3124, Australia

Penguin Books Canada Ltd, 10 Alcorn Avenue, Toronto, Ontario, Canada M4V 3B2

Penguin Books (N.Z.) Ltd, 182-190 Wairau Road, Auckland 10, New Zealand

First published in the United States of America by Dial Books for Young Readers,
a division of Penguin Putnam Inc., 1998
Published by Puffin Books,
a division of Penguin Putnam Books for Young Readers, 2000
This Puffin Modern Classics edition published by Puffin Books,
a division of Penguin Young Readers Group, 2004

5 7 9 10 8 6 4

Chapter 1, "Shotgun Cheatham's Last Night Above Ground," first appeared in
Twelve Shots: Stories About Guns edited by Harry Mazer, Delacorte Press
Books for Young Readers.
Copyright © Richard Peck, 1997

THE LIBRARY OF CONGRESS HAS CATALOGED THE DIAL EDITION AS FOLLOWS:

Peck, Richard, date.

A long way from Chicago: a novel in stories / by Richard Peck.—1st ed.

p.   cm.

Summary: A boy recounts his annual summer trips to rural Illinois with his sister
during the Great Depression to visit their larger-than-life grandmother.

ISBN: 0-8037-2290-7

[1. Grandmothers—Fiction. 2. Depressions—1929– —Fiction.

3. Country life—Fiction. 4. Illinois—Fiction.] 1. Title.

PZ7.P338Li 1998 [Fic]—DC21 98-10953 CIP AC

This edition ISBN 0-14-240110-2

Printed in the United States of America

*For Judy and David Everson
and to remember James Jones*

Contents

Prologue

It was always August when we spent a week with our grandma. I was Joey then, not Joe: Joey Dowdel, and my sister was Mary Alice. In our first visits we were still just kids, so we could hardly see her town because of Grandma. She was so big, and the town was so small. She was old too, or so we thought—old as the hills. And tough? She was tough as an old boot, or so we thought. As the years went by, though, Mary Alice and I grew up, and though Grandma never changed, we'd seem to see a different woman every summer.

Now I'm older than Grandma was then, quite a bit older. But as the time gets past me, I seem to remember more and more about those hot summer days and nights, and the last house in town, where Grandma lived. And Grandma. Are all my memories true? Every word, and growing truer with the years.

Shotgun Cheatham's
Last Night Above Ground

—•❧•—

1929

You wouldn't think we'd have to leave Chicago to see a dead body. We were growing up there back in the bad old days of Al Capone and Bugs Moran. Just the winter before, they'd had the St. Valentine's Day Massacre over on North Clark Street. The city had such an evil reputation that the Thompson submachine gun was better known as a "Chicago typewriter."

But I'd grown to the age of nine, and my sister Mary Alice was seven, and we'd yet to see a stiff. We guessed that most of them were where you couldn't see them, at the bottom of Lake Michigan, wearing concrete overshoes.

3

No, we had to travel all the way down to our Grandma Dowdel's before we ever set eyes on a corpse. Dad said Mary Alice and I were getting to the age when we could travel on our own. He said it was time we spent a week with Grandma, who was getting on in years. We hadn't seen anything of her since we were tykes. Being Chicago people, Mother and Dad didn't have a car. And Grandma wasn't on the telephone.

"They're dumping us on her is what they're doing," Mary Alice said darkly. She suspected that Mother and Dad would take off for a week of fishing up in Wisconsin in our absence.

I didn't mind going because we went on the train, the Wabash Railroad's crack Blue Bird that left Dearborn Station every morning, bound for St. Louis. Grandma lived somewhere in between, in one of those towns the railroad tracks cut in two. People stood out on their porches to see the train go through.

Mary Alice said she couldn't stand the place. For one thing, at Grandma's you had to go outside to the privy. It stood just across from the cobhouse, a tumbledown shed full of stuff left there in Grandpa Dowdel's time. A big old snaggletoothed tomcat lived in the cobhouse, and as quick as you'd come out of the privy, he'd jump at you. Mary Alice hated that.

Mary Alice said there was nothing to do and nobody to do it with, so she'd tag after me, though I was two years older and a boy. We'd stroll uptown in those first days. It was only a short block of brick buildings: the bank, the insurance agency, Moore's Store, and The Coffee Pot Cafe, where the old saloon had stood. Prohibition was on in those days, which meant that selling liquor was against the law. So people made their own beer at home. They still had the tin roofs out over the sidewalk, and hitching rails. Most farmers came to town horse-drawn, though there were Fords, and the banker, L. J. Weidenbach, drove a Hupmobile.

It looked like a slow place to us. But that was before they buried Shotgun Cheatham. He might have made it unnoticed all the way to the grave except for his name. The county seat newspaper didn't want to run an obituary on anybody called Shotgun, but nobody knew any other name for him. This sparked attention from some of the bigger newspapers. One sent in a stringer to nose around The Coffee Pot Cafe for a human-interest story since it was August, a slow month for news.

The Coffee Pot was where people went to loaf, talk tall, and swap gossip. Mary Alice and I were of some interest when we dropped by because we were kin of Mrs. Dowdel's, who never set foot in the place. She said she liked to keep herself to herself, which was uphill work in a town like that.

Mary Alice and I carried the tale home that a suspicious type had come off the train in citified clothes and a stiff straw hat. He stuck out a mile and was asking around about Shotgun Cheatham. And he was taking notes.

Grandma had already heard it on the grapevine that Shotgun was no more, though she wasn't the first person people ran to with news. She wasn't what you'd call a popular woman. Grandpa Dowdel had been well thought of, but he was long gone.

That was the day she was working tomatoes on the

black iron range, and her kitchen was hot enough to steam the calendars off the wall. Her sleeves were turned back on her big arms. When she heard the town was apt to fill up with newspaper reporters, her jaw clenched.

Presently she said, "I'll tell you what that reporter's after. He wants to get the horselaugh on us because he thinks we're nothing but a bunch of hayseeds and no-'count country people. We are, but what business is it of his?"

"Who was Shotgun Cheatham anyway?" Mary Alice asked.

"He was just an old reprobate who lived poor and died broke," Grandma said. "Nobody went near him because he smelled like a polecat. He lived in a chicken coop, and now they'll have to burn it down."

To change the subject she said to me, "Here, you stir these tomatoes, and don't let them stick. I've stood in this heat till I'm half-cooked myself."

I didn't like kitchen work. Yesterday she'd done apple butter, and that hadn't been too bad. She made that outdoors over an open fire, and she'd put pennies in the caldron to keep it from sticking.

"Down at The Coffee Pot they say Shotgun rode with the James boys."

"Which James boys?" Grandma asked.

"Jesse James," I said, "and Frank."

"They wouldn't have had him," she said. "Anyhow, them Jameses was Missouri people."

"They were telling the reporter Shotgun killed a man and went to the penitentiary."

"Several around here done that," Grandma said, "though

I don't recall him being out of town any length of time. Who's doing all this talking?"

"A real old, humped-over lady with buck teeth," Mary Alice said.

"Cross-eyed?" Grandma said. "That'd be Effie Wilcox. You think she's ugly now, you should have seen her as a girl. And she'd talk you to death. Her tongue's attached in the middle and flaps at both ends." Grandma was over by the screen door for a breath of air.

"They said he'd notched his gun in six places," I said, pushing my luck. "They said the notches were either for banks he'd robbed or for sheriffs he'd shot."

"Was that Effie again? Never trust an ugly woman. She's got a grudge against the world," said Grandma, who was no oil painting herself. She fetched up a sigh. "I'll tell you how Shotgun got his name. He wasn't but about ten years old, and he wanted to go out and shoot quail with a bunch of older boys. He couldn't hit a barn wall from the inside, and he had a sty in one eye. They were out there in a pasture without a quail in sight, but Shotgun got all excited being with the big boys. He squeezed off a round and killed a cow. Down she went. If he'd been aiming at her, she'd have died of old age eventually. The boys took the gun off him, not knowing who he'd plug next. That's how he got the name, and it stuck to him like fly-paper. Any girl in town could have outshot him, and that includes me." Grandma jerked a thumb at herself.

She kept a twelve-gauge double-barreled Winchester Model 21 behind the woodbox, but we figured it had been Grandpa Dowdel's for shooting ducks. "And I wasn't no Annie Oakley myself, except with squirrels." Grandma was still at the door, fanning her apron. Then in the same voice she said, "Looks like we got company. Take them tomatoes off the fire."

A stranger was on the porch, and when Mary Alice and I crowded up behind Grandma to see, it was the reporter. He was sharp-faced, and he'd sweated through his hatband.

"What's your business?" Grandma said through screen wire, which was as friendly as she got.

"Ma'am, I'm making inquiries about the late Shotgun Cheatham." He shuffled his feet, wanting to get one of them in the door. Then he mopped up under his hat brim with a silk handkerchief. His Masonic ring had diamond chips in it.

"Who sent you to me?"

"I'm going door-to-door, ma'am. You know how you ladies love to talk. Bless your hearts, you'd all talk the hind leg off a mule."

Mary Alice and I both stared at that. We figured Grandma might grab up her broom to swat him off the porch. We'd already seen how she could make short work of peddlers even when they weren't lippy. And tramps didn't seem to mark her fence post. We suspected that you didn't get inside her house even if she knew you. But to our surprise she swept open the screen door and stepped out onto the porch. I followed. So did Mary Alice, once she was sure the snaggletoothed tom wasn't lurking around out there, waiting to pounce.

"You a newspaper reporter?" she said. "Peoria?" It was

the flashy clothes, but he looked surprised. "What they been telling you?"

"Looks like I got a good story by the tail," he said. " 'Last of the Old Owlhoot Gunslingers Goes to a Pauper's Grave.' That kind of angle. Ma'am, I wonder if you could help me flesh out the story some."

"Well, I got flesh to spare," Grandma said mildly. "Who's been talking to you?"

"It was mainly an elderly lady—"

"Ugly as sin, calls herself Wilcox?" Grandma said. "She's been in the state hospital for the insane until just here lately, but as a reporter I guess you nosed that out."

Mary Alice nudged me hard, and the reporter's eyes widened.

"They tell you how Shotgun come by his name?"

"Opinions seem to vary, ma'am."

"Ah well, fame is fleeting," Grandma said. "He got it in the Civil War."

The reporter's hand hovered over his breast pocket, where a notepad stuck out.

"Oh yes, Shotgun went right through the war with the Illinois Volunteers. Shiloh in the spring of sixty-two, and he was with U. S. Grant when Vicksburg fell. That's where he got his name. Grant give it to him, in fact. Shotgun didn't hold with government-issue firearms. He shot rebels with his old Remington pump-action that he'd used to kill quail back here at home."

Now Mary Alice was yanking on my shirttail. We knew kids lie all the time, but Grandma was no kid, and she could tell some whoppers. Of course the reporter had been lied to big-time up at the cafe, but Grandma's lies were more interesting, even historical. They made Shotgun look better while they left Effie Wilcox in the dust.

"He was always a crack shot," she said, winding down. "Come home from the war with a line of medals bigger than his chest."

"And yet he died penniless," the reporter said in a thoughtful voice.

"Oh well, he'd sold off them medals and give the money to war widows and orphans."

A change crossed the reporter's narrow face. Shotgun had gone from kill-crazy gunslinger to war-hero marksman. Philanthropist, even. He fumbled his notepad out and was scribbling. He thought he'd hit pay dirt with Grandma. "It's all a matter of record," she said. "You could look it up."

He was ready to wire in a new story: "Civil War Hero Handpicked by U. S. Grant Called to the Great Campground in the Sky." Something like that. "And he never married?"

"Never did," Grandma said. "He broke Effie Wilcox's heart. She's bitter still, as you see."

"And now he goes to a pauper's grave with none to mark his passing," the reporter said, which may have been a sample of his writing style.

"They tell you that?" Grandma said. "They're pulling your leg, sonny. You drop by The Coffee Pot and tell them you heard that Shotgun's being buried from my house with full honors. He'll spend his last night above ground in my front room, and you're invited."

The reporter backed down the porch stairs, staggering under all this new material. "Much obliged, ma'am," he said.

"Happy to help," Grandma said.

Mary Alice had turned loose of my shirttail. What little we knew about grown-ups didn't seem to cover Grandma. She turned on us. "Now I've got to change my shoes and walk all the way up to the lumberyard in this heat," she said, as if she hadn't brought it all on herself. Up at the lumberyard they'd be knocking together Shotgun Cheatham's coffin and sending the bill to the county, and Grandma had to tell them to bring that coffin to her house, with Shotgun in it.

By nightfall a green pine coffin stood on two sawhorses in the bay window of the front room, and people milled in the yard. They couldn't see Shotgun from there because the coffin lid blocked the view. Besides, a heavy gauze hung from the open lid and down over the front of the coffin to veil him. Shotgun hadn't been exactly fresh when they discovered his body. Grandma had flung open every window, but there was a peculiar smell in the room. I'd only had one look at him when they'd carried in the coffin, and that was enough. I'll tell you just two things about him. He didn't have his teeth in, and he was wearing bib overalls.

The people in the yard still couldn't believe Grandma was holding open house. This didn't stop the reporter who was haunting the parlor, looking for more flesh to add to his story. And it didn't stop Mrs. L. J. Weidenbach, the banker's wife, who came leading her father, an ancient codger half her size in full Civil War Union blue.

"We are here to pay our respects at this sad time," Mrs. Weidenbach said when Grandma let them in. "When I told Daddy that Shotgun had been decorated by U. S. Grant and wounded three times at Bull Run, it brought it all back to him, and we had to come." Her old daddy wore a forage cap and a decoration from the Grand Army of the Republic, and he seemed to have no idea where he was. She led him up to the coffin, where they admired the flowers. Grandma had planted a pitcher of glads from her garden at either end of the pine box. In each pitcher she'd stuck an American flag.

A few more people willing to brave Grandma came and went, but finally we were down to the reporter, who'd settled into the best chair, still nosing for news. Then who appeared at the front door but Mrs. Effie Wilcox, in a hat.

"Mrs. Dowdel, I've come to set with you overnight and see our brave old soldier through his Last Watch."

In those days people sat up with a corpse through the final night before burial. I'd have bet money Grandma wouldn't let Mrs. Wilcox in for a quick look, let alone overnight. But of course Grandma was putting on the best show possible to pull wool over the reporter's eyes. Little though she seemed to think of townspeople, she thought less of strangers. Grandma waved Mrs. Wilcox inside, and in she came, her eyes all over the place. She made for the coffin, stared at the blank white gauze, and said, "Don't he look natural?"

Then she drew up a chair next to the reporter. He flinched because he had it on good authority that she'd just been let out of an insane asylum. "Warm, ain't it?" she said straight at him, but looking everywhere.

The crowd outside finally dispersed. Mary Alice and I hung at the edge of the room, too curious to be anywhere else.

"If you're here for the long haul," Grandma said to the reporter, "how about a beer?" He looked encouraged, and Grandma left him to Mrs. Wilcox, which was meant as a punishment. She came back with three of her home brews, cellar-cool. She brewed beer to drink herself, but these three bottles were to see the reporter through the night. She wouldn't have expected her worst enemy, Effie Wilcox, to drink alcohol in front of a man.

In normal circumstances the family recalls stories about the departed to pass the long night hours. But these circumstances weren't normal, and quite a bit had already been recalled about Shotgun Cheatham anyway.

Only a single lamp burned, and as midnight drew on, the glads drooped in their pitchers. I was wedged in a corner, beginning to doze, and Mary Alice was sound asleep on a throw rug. After the second beer the reporter lolled, visions of Shotgun's Civil War glories no doubt dancing in his head. You could hear the tick of the kitchen clock. Grandma's chin would drop, then jerk back. Mrs. Wilcox had been humming "Rock of Ages," but tapered off after "let me hide myself in thee."

Then there was the quietest sound you ever heard. Somewhere between a rustle and a whisper. It brought me around, and I saw Grandma sit forward and cock her head. I blinked to make sure I was awake, and the whole world seemed to listen. Not a leaf trembled outside.

But the gauze that hung down over the open coffin moved. Twitched.

Except for Mary Alice, we all saw it. The reporter sat bolt upright, and Mrs. Wilcox made a little sound.

Then nothing.

Then the gauze rippled as if a hand had passed across it from the other side, and in one place it wrinkled into a wad as if somebody had snagged it. As if a feeble hand had reached up from the coffin depths in one last desperate attempt to live before the dirt was shoveled in.

Every hair on my head stood up.

"Naw," Mrs. Wilcox said, strangling. She pulled back in her chair, and her hat went forward. "Naw!"

The reporter had his chair arms in a death grip. "Sweet mother of—"

But Grandma rocketed out of her chair. "Whoa, Shotgun!" she bellowed. "You've had your time, boy. You don't get no more!"

She galloped out of the room faster than I could believe. The reporter was riveted, and Mrs. Wilcox was sinking fast.

Quicker than it takes to tell, Grandma was back, and already raised to her aproned shoulder was the twelve-gauge Winchester from behind the woodbox. She swung it wildly around the room, skimming Mrs. Wilcox's hat, and took aim at the gauze that draped the yawning coffin. Then she squeezed off a round.

I thought that sound would bring the house down around us. I couldn't hear right for a week. Grandma roared out, "Rest in peace, you old—" Then she let fly with the other barrel.

The reporter came out of the chair and whipped completely around in a circle. Beer bottles went everywhere. The straight route to the front door was in Grandma's line of fire, and he didn't have the presence of mind to realize she'd already discharged both barrels. He went out a side window, headfirst, leaving his hat and his notepad behind. Which he feared more, the living dead or Grandma's aim, he didn't tarry to tell. Mrs. Wilcox was on her feet, hollering, "The dead is walking, and Mrs. Dowdel's gunning for me!" She cut and ran out the door and into the night.

When the screen door snapped to behind her, silence fell. Mary Alice hadn't moved. The first explosion had blasted her awake, but she naturally thought that Grandma had killed her, so she didn't bother to budge. She says the whole experience gave her nightmares for years after.

A burned-powder haze hung in the room, cutting the smell of Shotgun Cheatham. The white gauze was black rags now, and Grandma had blown the lid clear of the coffin. She'd have blown out all three windows in the bay, except they were open. As it was, she'd pitted her woodwork bad and topped the snowball bushes outside. But apart from scattered shot, she hadn't disfigured Shotgun Cheatham any more than he already was.

Grandma stood there savoring the silence. Then she turned toward the kitchen with the twelve-gauge loose in her hand. "Time you kids was in bed," she said as she trudged past us.

Apart from Grandma herself, I was the only one who'd seen her big old snaggletoothed tomcat streak out of the coffin and over the windowsill when she let fire. And I supposed she'd seen him climb in, which gave her ideas. It was the cat, sitting smug on Shotgun Cheatham's breathless chest, who'd batted at the gauze the way a cat will. And he sure lit out the way he'd come when Grandma fired just over his ragged ears, as he'd probably used up eight lives already.

The cat in the coffin gave Grandma Dowdel her chance. She didn't seem to have any time for Effie Wilcox, whose tongue flapped at both ends, but she had even less for newspaper reporters who think your business is theirs. Courtesy of the cat, she'd fired a round, so to speak, in the direction of each.

Though she didn't gloat, she looked satisfied. It certainly fleshed out her reputation and gave people new reason to leave her in peace. The story of Shotgun Cheatham's last night above ground kept The Coffee Pot Cafe fully engaged for the rest of our visit that summer. It was a story that grew in the telling in one of those little towns where there's always time to ponder all the different kinds of truth.

The Mouse in the Milk

1930

From something Dad said, it had dawned on Mary Alice and me that our trip down to Grandma's was meant to be an annual event.

Mary Alice pitched a fit. It meant another week of summer vacation away from her friends, Beverly and Audrey. Besides, she said she wasn't over last year's visit yet. One night she'd have a nightmare about old Shotgun Cheatham sitting up in his coffin, and on the night after that she'd dream that Grandma's big old tomcat was jumping at her. Or so she said.

But having no choice, we went. If any of us had grown over the year, it was Grandma herself. And she still seemed to prize her privacy as much as ever. She mostly stayed home because she said the whole town was a slum and she didn't give two hoots about it. And she wouldn't even have a radio in her house.

Mary Alice brought her jump rope to keep herself occupied, though she said jumping rope by yourself was the loneliest job in the world. I took a giant jigsaw puzzle to put together. It was supposed to depict Colonel Charles A. Lindbergh and his airplane, the *Spirit of St. Louis*. There wasn't room for it in our Chicago apartment. But in the summers Grandma took down the stove that heated her front room, so there was space to leave a card table up.

One night soon after we arrived, I was working on the puzzle and Grandma was drowsing in her platform rocker. She said she never slept, but she had to wake herself up to go to bed. Earlier, before it got dark, Mary Alice had been jumping rope outside. There weren't a lot of sidewalks in Grandma's town, but a strip of concrete ran from her front door out to the countrified mailbox beside the road. Grandma and I had been listening to Mary Alice:

> *Jump said Coolidge,*
> *Jump said Hoover,*
> *Jump said the driver of the furniture mover.*

And Mary Alice's personal favorite:

> *I had a letter from Nellie,*
> *And what do you think it said?*
> *Nellie had a baby,*
> *And its hair was red.*
> *Now how many hairs were on that head?*
> *One, two, three . . .*

When she got up to 180, Grandma called her inside.

So now Mary Alice was sulking somewhere. Grandma's breathing was steady, the way it got before she started snoring. Then I heard a horse clopping past.

That was no rare thing around here. But I noticed the silence when the horse stopped outside. Then right away heels kicked its sides, and the horse galloped off. It was a sound right out of a Tom Mix movie. I was reaching for a puzzle part that was just blue sky when a flash of light filled the bay window. Then an explosion shook the house and made my puzzle jump. It wasn't as loud as the time Grandma squeezed off two rounds right here in the front room. But it brought her out of her chair.

Like a ship under sail, she made for the front door. Mary Alice appeared from somewhere, and we both looked around Grandma into the night. You could barely see a stump out by the road. It was the post that had held the mailbox. But the mailbox was gone—in several directions. We heard a piece of metal slide down the shingles of the roof, bounce off the gutter, and fall through the snowball bushes.

Somebody on horseback had blown Grandma's mailbox sky high. The Fourth of July was over, but there were still plenty of loose fireworks around. And this was no small charge, not a baby-waker or even a torpedo. This could have been the work of a cherry bomb.

Grandma planted her big fists on her big hips, and her jaw clenched in a familiar way.

"Cowgills," she said, like that explained it.

Grandma slept in a room downstairs to save herself the stairs. Mary Alice and I had rooms upstairs. They were sparely furnished, with iron bedsteads and a lot of dead bugs on the sills. After I got used to how quiet the country was at night, I slept good up there. But I lay awake that night, recalling the sound when Grandma's mailbox was blown to smithereens. I was ten, the age when things blowing up interested me, but I wondered who'd dare do this to Grandma.

My eyelids drooped, and it was morning. The smell of breakfast wafted up from the kitchen. You had to be downstairs on time and in your place, but Grandma's breakfasts were worth it. Pancakes and corn syrup, fried ham and potatoes and onions, anything you wanted and as much.

Mary Alice and I were at the table, and Grandma was at the stove turning one last round of pancakes, when we got a visitor on the back porch. We all looked. The screen on the door blurred her, but it was Grandma's old enemy, Mrs. Effie Wilcox. She didn't make free to rap on the door. She just stood out on the porch in a faded apron and broken boots, working her hands. "Mrs. Dowdel, whoeee," she called out in a tragic voice.

Grandma strolled over to the door. "What now?" she said through screen wire.

Mrs. Wilcox moaned. "First of all," she said, "can I use it?"

She nodded down the back path to the cobhouse and the privy, and she didn't mean the cobhouse.

"Feel free," Grandma said. "Take a pew."

But Mrs. Wilcox just stood there on the porch, wringing her hands. "I'm so nervous, I don't know if—"

"What's come over you?" Grandma said in her least interested voice.

Mrs. Wilcox whimpered. "Send them kids out of your kitchen so I can tell you."

"They're having their breakfast," Grandma said, "and they're from Chicago, so they've heard everything."

"Well, it was last night," Mrs. Wilcox said. "They come on my place and wrenched up my you-know-what by the posts and flung it all over the yard."

"They knocked over your privy three months ahead of Halloween?" Grandma was interested at last. "What's the world coming to?"

"That's what I said," Mrs. Wilcox replied. "I'm too nervous to live. All the laws of civilization has broke down, and town life is getting too dangerous. My only consolation is that there's a prayer meeting at church tomorrow night. And I've got me some praying to do."

"Do that," Grandma said. But Mrs. Wilcox couldn't wait another minute. She darted off the porch and down the path to our privy.

Grandma settled into her chair to smother her last pancake with corn syrup. Then once again she said, "Cowgills."

Presently, Mary Alice slipped down from her chair and headed outside. When she got to the screen door, Grandma said, "I wouldn't use the privy all morning if I was you."

That next morning when I came into the kitchen, a sight stopped me dead in the door. Behind me, Mary Alice pulled up short too. Next to a box of shells, Grandpa Dowdel's old double-barreled Winchester Model 21 was on the kitchen table, along with a greasy rag, like Grandma meant to clean it. Just the sight of that gun made my ears ring. Then I saw somebody besides Grandma was in the kitchen, over by the door.

He was a big, tall galoot of a kid with narrow eyes. His gaze kept flitting to the shotgun. The uniform he had on was all white with a cap to match. In his hand was a wire holder for milk bottles. He was ready to make his escape, but Grandma was saying, "I hope I have better luck with your milk today than the last batch. I found a dead mouse in your delivery yesterday."

The kid's narrow eyes widened. "Naw you never," he said.

"Be real careful about calling a customer a liar," she remarked. "I had to feed that milk to the cat. And the mouse too, of course."

"Naw," the kid said, reaching around for the knob on the screen door behind him.

Grandma was telling one of her whoppers. If she'd found a mouse in the milk, she'd have exploded like the mailbox. She was telling a whopper, and I wondered why.

"And another thing," she said. "I won't be needing a delivery tomorrow, neither milk nor cream. I'm going away."

First we'd heard of it. Mary Alice nudged me hard.

"I'll be gone tonight and all day tomorrow, and I don't want the milk left out where it'll sour. I won't pay for it. I'm taking my grandkids on a visit to my cousin Leota Shrewsbury."

Another whopper, and a huge one. Grandma off on a jaunt and us with her? I didn't think so. She didn't do things that cost. And she never told anybody her business.

Turning from the stove, she pretended surprise at seeing Mary Alice and me there, though she had eyes in the back of her head. "Why, there's my grandkids now." She pointed us out with a spatula. "They're from Chicago. Gangs run that town, you know," she told the kid. "My grandson's in a gang, so you don't want to mess with him. He's meaner than he looks."

I hung in the doorway, bug-eyed and short. She was saying I—Joey Dowdel—was a tough guy from Chicago, and this kid was twice my size. He could eat me for lunch.

"This here's Ernie Cowgill," she said, finishing off the introductions. With a sneer at me, Ernie Cowgill disappeared through the door and stomped off the porch.

"Grandma," I croaked, "you'll get me killed."

She waved that away. "I just said that for your protection. He'll be scared of you now. He'd believe anything. He's only in fourth grade."

"Grandma, he's at least sixteen."

"That's right. And still in fourth grade," she said. "He's the runt of the Cowgill litter. He's got three older brothers, and they're big bruisers. They're the ones you wouldn't want to meet up with in a dark alley."

She swept shotgun, shells, and the greasy rag off the kitchen table and put them all back behind the woodbox. Then she nodded at Mary Alice to set the table for breakfast.

When we sat down to eat, I said, "Grandma, what was the shotgun for?"

"Bait," she said.

"Who's Cousin Leota Shrewsbury?" Mary Alice asked.

"Who?" Grandma said.

I lurked pretty near home all day. I didn't even go uptown to The Coffee Pot Cafe for fear I'd run into Ernie Cowgill and his brothers. Now I remembered where I'd heard the name. The horse-drawn milk wagon that delivered to the door had a sign on its side that read:

Cowgills' Dairy Farm

FROM OUR CLOVER-FED COWS TO YOUR KITCHEN
STRICTLY SANITARY
FARM-FRESH EGGS OUR SPECIALTY

In fact, I'd seen Ernie driving it standing up, handling the reins through a hole in the front window of the wagon. Even at a distance he looked like somebody you wouldn't want to know better.

It may have been just a coincidence that a family named Cowgill ran the dairy. I never knew.

Noticing how close to home I was keeping, Grandma told me to weed the garden. You didn't want to hang around her too close, or she'd give you a job. The garden ran neat and tidy from the back porch down to the cobhouse beside the yard where she stretched her clothesline. I weeded through the heat of the day, and every time I got down by the cobhouse, I had a vision of all four Cowgill brothers stepping out of it. I could picture them hanging me from the eaves by my belt and taking turns slapping me to sleep. But I saw nothing but the crossed paws of the old tomcat, napping just inside the door.

The two rows of green onions made my eyes water, and the smell was making me woozy. I was thinking seriously of heatstroke when I heard Mary Alice shriek in the kitchen. She was no screamer, so it brought me to my feet. Now I thought Ernie Cowgill had gotten in and pounced on her. I jumped the garden rows, pounding for the house.

But it was only Grandma and Mary Alice in the kitchen. Mary Alice's eyes were big as quarters, like Orphan Annie's, and she had both hands clapped over her mouth. Grandma towered over the table. Held high in her hand was a mouse-trap, with the mouse still in it. A good-sized mouse. Its tail dangled down so far, it looked like one of the flypaper strips that hung from her kitchen ceiling. The spring on the trap had caught the mouse at the neck and nearly pulled his head loose. He was hanging by a thread and not a pretty sight.

Mary Alice had already gone into shock. This was one more of those experiences she says gave her nightmares for years.

Grandma examined her catch. Now she moved the trap into position over the mouth of an empty bottle. She eased up the spring, and the mouse dropped straight in. He hit the bottom of the bottle with a soft thump.

She turned back to the drainboard and picked up another bottle, full of milk—fresh, I suppose, from Ernie Cowgill's morning delivery. Without spilling a drop, she poured milk into the bottle on the table. Mary Alice and I watched like two paralyzed people as the milk rose around the mouse's furry gray body until his whiskers began to float. As the milk closed over his head, Mary Alice bolted. If the back door had been latched, she'd have gone straight through screen wire.

Now Grandma was fitting a paper lid over the milk-and-mouse bottle. I knew not to ask why she was doing this. I didn't even want to know.

Mary Alice didn't come back in the house till supper time. Then she didn't want any supper. I watched her move green beans and fatback around the plate with the fork big in her small hand. Grandma ate hearty. After a big wedge of layer cake she pulled back from the table. "Let's step right along and get them dishes washed and dried and put up," she said. She was in a hurry, and I couldn't see why. But then I couldn't see a moment ahead.

There was still some evening left, but the light was fading. Grandma stayed in the kitchen after we'd wandered into the front room. But as Mary Alice was reaching for her jump rope to take outside, Grandma turned up and said, "Not tonight."

Mary Alice glowered but said nothing. She flopped on the settee and fidgeted. Then she started to go upstairs. She'd brought a book called *The Hidden Staircase* by Carolyn Keene, and she liked reading in bed. "Not tonight," Grandma said. She sat at her ease in the platform rocker, with her sewing basket at her feet. She didn't do much fancy needlework, but she mended everything. Mary Alice came over to lean against me while I worked on Colonel Lindbergh.

When it got so dark I couldn't see the puzzle, I reached to turn on the lamp. But Grandma said, "Not tonight."

By then we had to know we were in for something. "Shut the front door," Grandma told Mary Alice, who was just a little gray shape, mouselike, as she went over to close it. "And shoot the bolt across," said Grandma, who never locked her doors.

Now we three were only outlines in the dark parlor. Some plot was afoot. Mary Alice edged back on the settee. We were all waiting for something. It was dark now. I could picture what the house looked like from outside. Locked up, not a light showing upstairs or down. All of us gone away to visit Cousin Leota Shrewsbury, who didn't exist. Half an hour passed. Then Grandma spoke, making us leap. "We could tell ghost stories," she said.

"Not tonight," Mary Alice said in a small voice.

Later, much later, we heard something. The snowball bushes outside the window swayed gently. I barely saw Grandma's hand come up to stroke her cheek. We didn't breathe for listening.

Then footsteps on the back porch—creeping, then more confident. After all, nobody was home. A hand closed over the knob on the screen door to the kitchen, and found it latched.

We heard a little sawing, singing sound as a file began to slice through screen wire. From the settee Mary Alice made some tiny, terrified sound. Grandma reached down for something in her sewing basket. The darkness made me see pinwheels like sparklers. I just managed to notice Grandma's rocker was rocking and she wasn't in it. She was standing over me. "Keep just behind me," she whispered.

I followed her across the room to the kitchen. You wouldn't believe a woman that heavy could be so light on her feet. She floated, and we moved like some strange beast, big in front, small behind. Now we were by the door to the kitchen, and I heard the scuffle of heavy feet in there on the crinkly linoleum.

Grandma turned back to me. Under my nose she struck a wooden match with her thumbnail. Men strike a match one-handed, but you never see a woman doing that. She hid the flare of the flame with herself and touched the match to something in her other hand. It sizzled. Then she leaned down and rolled it into the invisible kitchen.

Seconds passed. Then once more, Grandma's house erupted in sound and light. Blue lightning flashed in the kitchen, and for a split second you could see every calendar on the wall in there. Then an almighty explosion like the crack of doom. She'd rolled a cherry bomb across the floor, and it went off right under the eight feet of the Cowgill brothers, the three big bruisers and Ernie.

Grandma shoved me past her into the kitchen. "Pull the chain on the ceiling light," she said, and I did. When I turned back to her, Grandpa Dowdel's shotgun was wedged into her shoulder. I dodged out of her way, and there stood all four Cowgill brothers. They were deaf as posts and too scared to move, even before they realized they were looking down both barrels of the gun they'd come to steal.

All of them wore manure-caked steel-toed boots, so that had saved their toes from being blown off. But a singed smell came from their pants. The cherry bomb had scared them witless, except for Ernie, who was witless anyway. But he was the only one who could speak. "I'm dead," he said. "I'm dead. Oh yes, I'm dead."

"Skin to the church and get their maw and paw," Grandma said briefly to me.

"Which church?"

"Holy Rollers," she said. "By the lumberyard. And step on it. I've got an itchy trigger finger."

"I'm dead," Ernie said.

I raced like the wind through the nighttime town. I sprinted past the business block and across the tracks by the depot toward the lumberyard. Then I began to hear singing with a ragtime beat, accompanied by tambourines:

> *Wash me clean of all I've been*
> *And hang me out to dry;*
> *Purify me, thought and deed,*
> *That I may dwell on high!*

The church was no bigger than a one-room schoolhouse, but it seemed to be packed to the rafters. The rail outside was thick with horses hitched to wagons. One of the wagons was from Cowgills' Dairy Farm.

Light and song were pouring out of the open doorway. I stood in it, remembering I didn't know what the

Cowgills' maw and paw looked like. Besides, all I could see were the backs of peoples' heads. Then I got lucky. Mrs. Effie Wilcox sat at the end of a pew. I knew her from her hat. Her hands were high above her head, swaying in the air, and she was singing with the rest:

> Drive the devil from my soul,
> Tie him to a tree;
> Let me rise into the skies
> That I may dwell with Thee!

I sidled down the side aisle, breathing heavy. Every minute counted, and I didn't know how long this hymn might last. It sounded like it could have a lot of verses.

> Hate the sin, but love the sinner,
> Though let him feel the rod;
> Lift me like a little child
> That I may dwell with—

I tapped Mrs. Wilcox on the shoulder. She jerked around. "It's a miracle," she hollered out. "The first Dowdel ever seen in the House of the Lord! Hallelujah, one more sinner gathered in!"

"Listen, Mrs. Wilcox," I said, urgent in her ear. "Where are the Cowgills? It's kind of important."

"The Cowgills?" she said. "Why, they're right here next to me. Where else would they be? They been saved, and now you—"

"Listen, Mrs. Wilcox. Grandma blew up all four of their

boys with a cherry bomb. Now she's got them pinned down with the shotgun."

Mrs. Wilcox's mouth opened in a silent scream.

Then all four of us, Mr. and Mrs. Cowgill, Mrs. Wilcox, and me, were in the swaying milk wagon behind the galloping horse. There aren't any seats in a milk wagon, so we clung to the sides and each other. For somebody too nervous to live, Mrs. Wilcox stood the trip pretty well.

The wagon bounced across Grandma's side yard. Now we were all tumbling down and racing each other to the back door. To keep up, both ladies held their skirts high. We burst into the kitchen, and it seemed that nobody had moved a muscle in there. The butt of the shotgun was still buried in Grandma's shoulder, and she was squinting down the barrels. The Cowgill boys looked like they were on the chain gang already.

I got my first real look at their maw and paw. She was kind of a faded lady, and he had a milder look than his bruiser boys. They were all a lot taller than he was.

"Now, now," Mr. Cowgill said, "what have we here?"

"What we have here," Grandma said, "is breaking-and-entering. Burglary and pilfering. Reform school for the youngest one, the penitentiary for the overgrown ones. Unless my trigger finger gives way to temptation. They wanted this shotgun, and they're liable to get it, right between the eyes."

The ceiling light glinted wickedly off her spectacles. "And they tore down Effie Wilcox's specialty house. Tell it, Effie. You knew at the time who the culprits was who kicked your privy to kingdom come."

Mrs. Wilcox whimpered.

"Now, now, Mrs. Dowdel," Mr. Cowgill said. "This is nothing more than a misunderstanding. My boys aren't broke out with brains, you know. I have an idea they just wandered into the wrong house."

"Oh, they wandered into the wrong house all right," Grandma said. "And they'd already blowed up the wrong mailbox."

"Mrs. Dowdel, Mrs. Dowdel, compose your soul in patience," Mr. Cowgill said. "And put up that shotgun. It don't look ladylike."

I was tempted to cover my ears, because that alone was enough to make Grandma squeeze off a round. "You know yourself, Mrs. Dowdel, boys will be boys. They's high-spirited. They'll settle down in time and all be good Christian men. Their maw and I have set them a good example."

I thought Mr. Cowgill was going way out on a limb. But strangely, Grandma lowered the shotgun. "Well, you know best, being their paw," she said calmly. She stood the shotgun against the wall and folded her arms before her. "But get them out of my kitchen, and you owe me for the screen wire they cut to get in. And I'll want me a new mailbox. A good galvanized iron one, even if it runs you three dollars."

Mr. Cowgill paled at that, but said, "There now. I knew you'd see sense, Mrs. Dowdel. Boys go through these phases. Come along, boys." He patted his biggest bruiser's shoulder, and all four of them were trying hard not to smirk. Mrs. Cowgill left first, supported by Mrs.

Wilcox. Then the bruisers and Ernie trooped out. Their paw was just at the door when Grandma said, "Not so fast, Cowgill."

He turned, unwilling, back.

"I'll be interested in your explanation for that." She pointed to the milk bottle that nobody had noticed, though it stood on the kitchen table.

The milk in it was more pink than white now. But you could see the mouse inside. In fact, it had swelled up some.

"What the—"

"You can say that again," Grandma remarked.

Sweat popped out on Mr. Cowgill's brow. "Mrs. Dowdel, you don't mean to tell me—"

"I don't mean to tell you a thing. There stands the evidence."

"Mrs. Dowdel, it can't be. We're strictly sanitary. We strain our milk." Sweat ran in rivers off his pate.

"I don't doubt it," she said. "After all, you've got to keep your good name in a town like this."

"Then how—"

"A bunch of worthless boys who'd ransack the town every night is apt to drop a mouse in the milk just before delivering to my door. Your big ones is perfectly capable of putting Ernie up to it. He's simple. After all, they blew up my mailbox, and Effie Wilcox has to use my privy. Thugs like yours who prey on two old helpless widow women such as Effie and myself is liable to get up to anything. Many more mice in the milk, and your customers will start keeping their own cows again."

Mr. Cowgill shrank. His dry mouth worked wordlessly, and there was fear in his eyes, naked fear. He didn't mind what his boys did to the town, but now he saw his business going down the drain, so to speak.

"Mrs. Dowdel," he said in a broken voice. "What do you want?"

"Justice," Grandma said.

A pause fell upon them. Grandma and Mr. Cowgill seemed to have a moment of complete understanding.

Then he said, "What'll I use?"

She nodded across the kitchen to the sink. In his earthly life Grandpa Dowdel had shaved over that sink. The mirror still hung there from his time, and beside it a long leather strop for sharpening the edge on his cutthroat razor.

Mr. Cowgill edged around the kitchen table and pulled the strop off the wall. Then he left. Grandma and I filled the doorway to watch.

It was dark out there, but you could see the lumpish shapes of the Cowgill boys hanging around the milk wagon, waiting for their paw. They didn't have to wait a minute more.

"Line up according to age," he called out, snapping the long leather strop above his head. Then he whaled the tar out of every one of them. They squealed like stuck hogs while Mrs. Cowgill lamented from the milk wagon. He took each by the arm in turn and gave them all what for. You could tell when he got to Ernie because a wavering voice cried out, "I'm dead."

At last the milk wagon clattered out of the yard. Grandma stayed at the door as peace descended. The snap of the strop against bruiser britches seem to linger in the night air. Mary Alice joined us. She'd made herself scarce once she'd seen Grandma grab up the shotgun. She was a little older now, a little wiser.

Then back up the path came Mrs. Wilcox. You could see the shape of her hat bobbing against the dark. She'd been making a call at our privy on her way home.

"Night now," she called out, crossing the yard.

"Night, Effie," Grandma called back to her worst enemy.

Then she turned from the door, and I saw the look on her face. You had to study hard to see any expression at all, but it was a look I was coming to know. She appeared pretty satisfied at the way things had turned out. And she'd returned law and order to the town she claimed she didn't give two hoots about.

A One-Woman Crime Wave

—⟨∾∾⟩—

1931

A Great Depression had swept over the nation, and we couldn't seem to throw it off. It was still Hoovering over us, as people said. It hadn't bottomed out yet, but it was heading that way.

You could see hard times from the window of the Wabash Blue Bird. The freight trains on the siding were loaded down with men trying to get from one part of the country to another, looking for work and something to eat. Mary Alice and I watched them as they stood in the open doors of the freight cars. They were walking along the right-of-way too, with nothing in their hands.

Then when we got off the train at Grandma's, a new sign on the platform read:

But at Grandma's house it seemed to be business as usual. Mary Alice was still skittish about the old snaggletoothed tomcat in the cobhouse. Grandma said if he worried her that much, she ought to use the chamber pot in place of the privy. Chamber pots were under all the beds, and they were handy at night. But Mary Alice wouldn't use hers during the day. She didn't want to climb the stairs just for that. And she didn't want to have to empty it any more than necessary.

Being nine, Mary Alice decided to take charge. She carried a broom to the privy, to swat the cat if it gave her any trouble. She was soon back that first afternoon, dragging the broom. Her eyes were watering, and she was holding her nose. "Something died in the cobhouse," she said.

"Naw," Grandma said. "It's cheese."

"I don't want any," Mary Alice said.

"It's not for you," Grandma said.

Now that they mentioned it, I could smell something pretty powerful wafting into the kitchen. And I could see the old tomcat from here, stretched out in the yard. He was breathing hard and nowhere near the cobhouse. The cheese smelled bad enough to gas a cat, but it was no use asking what it was for. We were bound to find out.

Grandma's house was the last one in town. Next to the row of glads was a woven-wire fence, and on the other side of that a cornfield. On the first nights I'd always lie up in bed, listening to the husky whisper of the dry August corn in the fields. Then on the second night I wouldn't hear anything.

But this year came the sound of shuffling boots and sometimes a voice. The Wabash tracks that cut the town in two ran along the other side of the road. The sheriff's deputies were out, carrying shotguns, moving the drifters along, so they didn't hang around town to beg for food. From my window I watched the swaying lanterns, and ahead of them the slumping figures of the drifters, heading for the next town. It was kind of spooky, and sad.

But it was a short night. At five the next morning Grandma was at the foot of the stairs, banging a spoon against a pan. When we got down to the kitchen, we found her in a pair of men's overalls stuffed into gum boots. She couldn't go outdoors in overalls, so she'd pulled a wash dress on over them, and her apron over that. Crowning it all was her gardening hat. She'd anchored it with a veil to keep the mosquitoes away, and tied it under her chins. She looked like a moving mountain. Mary Alice couldn't believe the overalls.

"Keeps off the chiggers," Grandma explained. "We're going fishing."

I looked around for the rods and reels, at least some bamboo poles, but didn't see anything.

"It's just one thing after another in town," Grandma declared. "We wasn't over Decoration Day before it was the Fourth of July. Then come the Old Settlers' picnic. You can't hardly get down the street for the crowds, and the dust never settles. I need me a day off and some peace and quiet."

Fresh from the Chicago Loop, Mary Alice and I traded glances.

We didn't linger over breakfast because of the smell. The cheese was on the back porch now, in a gunnysack. It began to dawn on me that it was the kind of cheese catfish consider a delicacy.

Grandma was ready to go, and when she was ready, you'd better be. "Let's get on the road," she said, taking a last look around the kitchen. "Douse the fire and hide the ax and skillet."

We blinked.

"Just a saying," Grandma said. "A country saying. I was a country girl, you know."

She carried the gunnysack of cheese herself, tied to the end of a tree limb hitched up on her shoulder. I was in charge of the picnic hamper, and it took all I had to lift it. I looked inside. Half the hamper was home-canned fruit: tomatoes and pickled peaches. The other half was vegetables from her garden: snap beans, four turnips, a cabbage. The only thing that looked like a picnic was a loaf of unsliced, home-baked bread. But I didn't ask. Grandma saved herself a lot of bother by not being the kind of person you question.

We trooped out into the morning behind her. As soon as we left her yard, we were in the country, but I had the feeling it could be a long trip. The hamper weighed a ton, and I had no luck in getting Mary Alice to carry the other handle.

We were well covered against chiggers, and the day was already too hot. Mary Alice preferred skirts, but she had on her playsuit with the long pants. Being eleven, I was way too old for shorts anyway, so I had on my jeans. We marched behind Grandma, and it wasn't too bad until the sun came up over the tassels on the corn.

We ate the dust of the road for a mile or so. Of course being a city boy, I didn't know what a mile was, but it felt like a mile. At a stand of timber we veered across a pasture.

"Watch your step," Grandma said. "Cow pies aplenty."

We were making for Salt Creek, and pretty soon the trees along the creek began to show on the horizon. But they were like a mirage that keeps its distance.

Finally we came to a barbed-wire fence with a sign on it:

NO TRESPASSING WHATSOEVER
NO FISHING, NOTHIN
PRIVATE PROPERTY
OF
PIATT COUNTY ROD & GUN CLUB
(SIGNED) O. B. DICKERSON, SHERIFF

"Lift that wire so I can skin under," Grandma said.

The lowest wire was pretty close to the ground. But Grandma was already flat on her back in the weeds. She'd pushed the cheese through. Now she began to work her shoulders to inch herself under. I pulled up on the wire to the best of my ability, but there wasn't much slack to it. The barbs snagged her hat, though they cleared her nose. But now here came her bosom. Mary Alice stood by, sucking in her own small chest, hoping to help. The wire cut my hand, and I was stabbed three times by the barbs. But like a miracle, Grandma shimmied under. Mary Alice followed with plenty of room, though she didn't like to get burrs in her hair.

Being a boy, I climbed the wires and pivoted over on a fence post, on the heel of my wounded hand. I dragged the hamper through, and now we were in forbidden territory. It all looked overgrown and deserted to me. But Grandma, speaking low, said, "Hush up from here on, and keep just behind me."

We were in trees and tall grass. As we sloped to the creek bottoms, the ground grew soggy underfoot. Dragonflies skated over the scum on the stagnant backwater. Grandma made her way along the willows weeping into the water. When she pulled back a tangle of vines, we saw an old, worn-out, snub-nosed rowboat. It was pulled up and tied to a tree, and the oars were shipped in the wet bottom, beside a long pole with a steel hook at the end.

"Work that rope loose," Grandma whispered to me. She pointed for Mary Alice to climb aboard, and she followed, reaching back to me for the hamper. The knot was easy, but pushing the boat out with Grandma in it wasn't. By the time the boat was afloat, I was up to my shoetops in muddy water.

I never thought for a minute that this was Grandma's boat. But she was one expert rower. She had the oars in the locks, and they pulled the water with hardly a ripple. She turned us and rowed along the bank, under the low-hanging limbs. We were on our way somewhere, quiet as the morning.

I was in the back of the boat, lolling, my mind drifting. Then I got the scare of my life. A low limb writhed and looped. I caught a quick glimpse of sliding scales and an evil eye, maybe a fang. Then an enormous snake dropped into the boat.

It just missed Grandma's lap and fell hissing between her and me. The last thing I saw was this thing, thick as a tire, snapping into a coil.

When I came to, we were tied up to a sapling, and Grandma was crouched over me. She was applying a rag wet with creek water to my forehead. Mary Alice was behind her, looking round-eyed at me.

"You fainted, Joey," she accused.

Boys don't faint. I passed out, and it was probably mostly the heat. Sunstroke maybe. Then I remembered the snake and grabbed up my knees.

"Never mind," Grandma said. "It's gone. It was harmless. Good-sized, but harmless. There's cottonmouths around though, so I'd keep my hands in the boat if I was you."

"It was swell," Mary Alice said. "It was *keen*. You should have seen how Grandma grabbed it up by its tail and snapped it just once and broke its neck."

It was all neck, if you asked me.

"Then she hauled off and flung it way out in the water," Mary Alice went on relentlessly. "Grandma's something with snakes. You should have seen—"

"Okay, okay," I muttered. Grandma stifled a rare smile. I suspected she had no high opinion of the bravery of the male sex, and I hadn't done anything to change her mind. Why wasn't it Mary Alice who'd done the fainting? It bothered me off and on for years.

We were under way again, me keeping a sharp eye on low-hanging limbs. I was recovering from everything but embarrassment, and Grandma was rowing out from the bank. Now she was putting up the oars and standing in the boat. It rocked dangerously, though she planted her big boots as wide as the sides allowed. She reached down for the long rod with the hook at the end.

Glancing briefly into the brown water, she plunged the rod into the creek. It hit something, and she began to pull the rod back up, hand over hand. She was weaving to keep her balance in the tipping boat. I wanted to hang on to the sides, but pictured a cottonmouth rearing up and sinking fangs in my hand.

Something broke the surface of the creek, something on a chain Grandma had hooked. It was bigger than the picnic hamper and looked like an orange crate, streaming water. And inside: whipping tails and general writhing.

I thought of cottonmouths and ducked. But they were catfish, mad as hornets, who'd been drawn by Grandma's terrible cheese. She heaved in the crate and unlatched the top. In the bottom of the boat was a wire-and-net contraption that expanded as she filled it with wiggling fish. A catfish is the ugliest thing with gills, and even Mary Alice drew back her feet. Grandma kept at it, bent double in the boat. She was as busy as a bird dog, one of her own favorite sayings. When all the catfish were in the net, flopping their last in the bottom of the boat, she took the new cheese out of the gunnysack and stuck it in the crate.

"Grandma, how did you remember where it was?" I said, amazed. "You couldn't see it, but you snagged it with the hook right off."

"Remembered where I'd sunk it," she said briefly. Now she was lowering the empty crate, baited with cheese, back in the water. Except it wasn't a crate. It was a fish trap. Where we went in Wisconsin to fish, using a fish trap carried a five-dollar fine.

"Grandma," I said, "is trapping fish legal in this state?"

"If it was," she said, "we wouldn't have to be so quiet."

"What's the fine?"

"Nothin' if you don't get caught," she said. "Anyhow, it's not my boat." Which was an example of the way Grandma reasoned. "Them critters love that cheese," she said fondly as the trap sank from view. She bent over the side to try to wash the smell off her hands, nearly swamping the boat.

Soon we were gliding gently downstream, Grandma rowing easy. The catfish were at her feet, flopping less now.

My brain buzzed. Dad was a dedicated fisherman. He tied his own flies. He was a member of the Conservation Club. What if he knew his own mother ran illegal fish traps? Brewing home beer was one thing, because the Prohibition law only profited the bootleggers. But we're talking about good sportsmanship here.

I noticed Mary Alice's eyes on me. She was watching me around Grandma's rowing arm, and she was reading my mind. It was then we decided never to tell Dad.

You could say one thing for Grandma's method. You got all your fishing done at once. It wasn't later than eight o'clock, and maybe we'd gotten away with it. It seemed to me we ought to have brought some poles along, and a can of worms, considering our catch. But I thought maybe things would settle down now, and we could have the quiet day in the country Grandma wanted. Then we heard singing.

I almost jumped out of the boat. It had felt as if we three were alone in the world. Now this singing warbled up from around a bend in the creek, like a bad barbershop quartet with extra voices chiming in:

> *Camptown ladies sing this song,*
> *Doo-dah, doo-dah. . . .*

Grandma nudged the boat into the bank just where the creek began to bend. Through the undergrowth we saw a ramshackle building on the far bank. Above the porch was a sign, a plank with words burned in:

ROD & GUN CLUB

A row of empty whisky bottles stood on the porch rail and from behind them came the singing:

Bet my money on the bobtail nag,
Somebody bet on the bay.

The porch sagged with singers—grown men in their underwear, still partying from last night. Old guys in real droopy underwear. It was a grisly sight, and Mary Alice's eyes bugged. I wasn't sure she ought to be seeing this. They were waving bottles and trying to dance. I didn't know what they'd do next. Grandma was fascinated.

As we watched, a skinny old guy with a deputy's badge pinned to his long johns stepped forth and was real sick over the rail into the water.

"Earl T. Askew," Grandma muttered, "president of the Chamber of Commerce."

But now a fat old geezer in the droopiest drawers and nothing else pulled himself up on the porch rail. Bottles toppled into the water as he stood barefoot on the rail, teetering back, then forward, while the others behind him roared, "Whoa, whoa."

"Shut up a minute," he roared back at them, "and I'll sing you a *good* song." He took a slug out of the bottle in his fist, and began:

> *The night that Paddy Murphy died*
> *I never shall forget.*
> *The whole durn town got stinkin' drunk,*
> *And some ain't sober yet.*
> *The only thing they done that night*
> *That filled my heart with fear,*
> *They took the ice right off the corpse*
> *And put it in the beer.*

Then he fell back into the arms of the cheering crowd.

"Ain't that disgusting?" Grandma said. "He couldn't carry a tune in a bucket."

"Who is he?" I whispered.

"O. B. Dickerson, the sheriff," she said, "and them drunk skunks with him is the entire business community of the town."

Mary Alice gasped. The drawers on some of the business community were riding mighty low. "They're not acting right," she said, very prim.

"Men in a bunch never do," Grandma said.

They were tight enough to fight too, and we were on their private property. Not only that. We were in a boat full of trapped fish almost under the bloodshot eye of the sheriff. I thought it was time to head upstream as fast as Grandma could row.

But no. She jammed an oar into the bank to push us off. Then she began rowing around the bend. My heart stopped. The full chorus was singing again, louder as we got nearer.

Sweet Adeline, old pal of mine. . . .

The Rod & Gun Club came into view, and so did we. Mary Alice was perched in the bow. Grandma was rowing steady, and I was in the stern, wondering if the fish showed.

It took the drunks on the porch a moment to focus on us. We were sailing right past them now, smooth as silk, big as life.

They saw us.

And Grandma saw them, as if for the first time. She seemed to lose control of the oars, and her mouth fell open in shock. Mary Alice was already shocked and didn't have to pretend. I didn't know where to look.

Some of the business community were so far gone, they just stared back, unbelieving. They thought they owned this stretch of the creek. A few, seeing that Grandma and Mary Alice were of the opposite sex, scrambled to hide themselves behind the others.

But you never saw anybody looking as scandalized as Grandma was at these old birds in their union suits and less. She was speechless as her gaze passed over them all, recognizing everybody.

It was a silent scene until Sheriff O. B. Dickerson found his voice. "Stop in the name of the law!" he bellowed. "That's my boat!"

Before the Rod & Gun Club was out of sight, Grandma had regained control of the oars. She rowed on as if none of this had ever happened. The sun was beating down, so she didn't push herself. After all, the sheriff couldn't chase us downstream. We were in his boat.

Around another bend and a flock of turtles sunning on stumps, Grandma pulled for the remains of an old dock. We tied up there, and now we were out of the boat, climbing a bluff. Grandma led, dragging the net of catfish. I was in the rear, doing my best with the picnic hamper. Mary Alice was between us, watching where she walked. She was scareder of snakes than she let on, if you ask me.

An old house without a speck of paint on it stood tall on the bluff. Its outbuildings had caved in, and the privy stood at an angle. There were still prairie chickens around in those days, and they were pecking dirt. Otherwise, the place looked lifeless. Rags hung at the windows.

The porch overlooking the creek had fallen off. Grandma tramped around to the far side of the house. She dropped her fish on the ground and waved us inside. Even in full daylight the place looked haunted. I didn't want to go in, but Mary Alice was marching through the door already. So I had to. "Is anybody inside?" I whispered to Grandma as I lugged the hamper past her.

"Nobody but Aunt Puss Chapman," she said, like anybody would know that.

It had been a fine house once. A wide black walnut staircase rose to a landing window with most of its stained glass still in. But it was creepy in here, dim and dusty. Smelled funny too. We went into a room piled up with furniture. Then one of the chairs spoke.

"Where you been, girl?"

Mary Alice flinched, but the old woman lost in the chair was staring straight at Grandma. And calling her *girl*?

She was by many years the oldest person we'd ever seen up till then. Bald as an egg, but she needed a shave. And not a tooth in her head.

"Who's them chilrun with you?" she demanded of Grandma.

"Just kids I found along the crick bank," Grandma said, to our surprise. "They was fishing."

"I don't know as I want them in the house." Aunt Puss Chapman sent us a mean look. "Do they steal?"

"Nothin' you've got," Grandma said, under her breath.

"Talk up, girl," Aunt Puss said. "You mumble. I've spoken to you about that before." She pulled her shawl closer, though it was the hottest day of the year. "I'm hongry. You hightailed it out of here after breakfast, and I ain't seen hide nor hoof mark of you since."

"She ain't seen me for a week," Grandma mumbled to us. "But she forgets."

Then she called out to Aunt Puss: "Catfish and fried potatoes and onions, vinegar slaw, and a pickled peach apiece. And more of the same for your supper."

"I suppose it beats starving," Aunt Puss snapped. "But hop to it, girl. Stir yer stumps."

I thought I might faint again. Nobody could talk to Grandma like that and live.

She led us back to an old-time kitchen. It was in bad shape, but well stocked: big sacks of potatoes and onions, cornmeal, things in cans. And we'd brought a full hamper to add to Aunt Puss's larder.

I had to fire up the stove with a bunch of kindling while Grandma and Mary Alice went to work on the potatoes and onions. Mary Alice was in as big a daze as I was. "Grandma, is that nasty old lady your aunt?"

I stopped to listen. If she was, that made her our great-great-aunt.

"Naw, I was hired girl to her before I was married,"

Grandma said. "Lived in this house and fetched and carried for her and slept in the attic."

"You had a room in the attic?"

"Naw, I just slept up there. Had a bed tick with straw in it and changed it every spring. I haven't always lived in the luxury you see me in now."

"What did she pay you, Grandma?"

"Pay? She didn't pay me a plug nickel. But she fed me."

I thought about that.

"And now you feed her," I said, but Grandma didn't reply.

We cleaned the fish on a plank table outdoors. I didn't care much for it. It made me kind of sick to hear Grandma rip the skin off the catfish. She had her own quick way of doing that. But every time, it sounded like the fish screamed. She put me in charge of chopping off their heads, but I didn't like chopping off the head of anything looking back at me. And catfish have mustaches for some reason, which is just plain weird. Finally, Mary Alice took the rusty hatchet out of my hand. And *whomp,* she'd bring down the blade, and that fish head would go flying. Mary Alice was good at it, so I let her do it. Grandma gutted.

It was afternoon before we sat down at the dining-room table under a cobwebby gasolier. Aunt Puss was already at her place, so she was spryer than she looked. Grandma settled at the foot of the table. Without her hat, her white hair hung in damp tendrils. We'd been working like a whole pack of bird dogs.

Watching Aunt Puss gum catfish was not a pretty

sight. "These fish taste muddy," she observed. "You'uns catch 'em?"

"Yes," I said.

"No," Mary Alice said.

"What did you use for bait?" Aunt Puss said, looking at both of us.

"Cheese," I said.

"Worms," Mary Alice said, more wisely.

Since we couldn't get together on our story, Aunt Puss changed the subject. "You chilrun still in school?"

We nodded.

"Do they whup you?"

"Do they what?" Mary Alice said.

"Do they paddle yer behind when you need it?" Aunt Puss looked interested.

"If they did, I'd quit school," said Mary Alice, who'd just completed third grade.

"They whupped that girl raw." Aunt Puss pointed her fork down the table at Grandma.

I had a sudden thought. Aunt Puss thought Grandma and Mary Alice and I were all about the same age. She hadn't noticed the years passing. That's why Grandma didn't say we were her grandkids. It would just have mixed up Aunt Puss.

"That's when she come to work for me. They'd throwed her out of school." Aunt Puss peered down the table. "Tell 'em why."

We looked at Grandma, naturally interested to know why she'd been throwed—thrown out of school. Grandma waved us away. "I forget," she said.

"I don't!" Aunt Puss waved a fork. "It was because you wadded up your underdrawers to stop up the flue on the stove and smoke out the schoolhouse. That was the end of yer education!"

"Working for *you* was an education," Grandma muttered, though only Mary Alice and I heard.

It took us another hour to clean up the kitchen the way Grandma wanted to leave it. When it was time for us to go, Aunt Puss was back in her chair in the parlor.

"Where do you think you're off to now?" she called out as we trooped through the front hall.

"Down to the sty to slop the hogs," Grandma called back.

"Well, don't dawdle. You dawdle, and I've spoken to you about that before. Get on out of here," Aunt Puss hollered. "Let the door hit you where the dog bit you."

Outdoors I said, "Does she have hogs?"

"She used to," Grandma said. "She was right well-off at one time. She's poor now, but she don't know it."

How could she? She still had her hired girl and plenty to eat.

"You take her food every week, don't you, Grandma?"

"Generally a good big roast chicken. She can gum that for days." Grandma turned down the lane. "It keeps her out of the poor farm, and it gives me a quiet day in the country. That's a fair swap." Then her jaw clenched in its way. "But it's just private business between her and me. And I don't tell my private business."

We walked country roads all the way home. Grandma set

a brisk pace, and I struggled along behind with a hamper heavy with cleaned catfish. Mary Alice went in the middle, watching where she walked.

By the time we got home, the trees in Grandma's yard were throwing long shadows, and it was evening in her kitchen. Mary Alice and I were both staggering. I was ready to go straight up to bed.

But Grandma said, "Skin down to the cellar and bring up fifteen or twenty bottles of my beer. Just carry two at a time. I don't want any broke."

I whimpered.

But she was turning on Mary Alice. "And you and me's going to fry up a couple pecks of potatoes to go with the fish. There won't be nothing to it. I peeled the potatoes this morning before you two was up."

We stared.

The catfish fried in long pans with the potatoes and onions at the other end, popping in the grease. The kitchen was blue with smoke, and night was at the windows before we finished up. "Now get down every platter I own," she told me. Then she sent me for the card table I'd used for my jigsaw puzzle of Charles A. Lindbergh.

Following her lead, we carried everything out into the night, making many trips. We lugged it all across the road and up to the Wabash Railroad right-of-way and planted the card table in the gravel.

Finally, the platters of fish and potatoes overlapped on the table, and the opened beer bottles stood in a row beside the tracks.

As the drifters came along, being hounded out of town,

Grandma gave them a good feed and a beer to wet their whistles. Mary Alice helped, in an apron of Grandma's that dragged the ground. They were hollow-eyed men who couldn't believe their luck. Two or three of them, then five or six. Then a bunch, standing around the table, eating with both hands, sharing out the beer. They didn't say much. They didn't thank her. She wasn't looking for thanks.

She'd taken off her overalls and put the same wash dress back on, but she'd tied a fresh apron over it. Her hair was a mess, fanning out from the bun at the back, white in the moonlight. She watched them feed, working her mouth.

Then we saw the swinging lanterns, the sheriff and his deputies coming along behind to keep the drifters moving.

Up trooped O. B. Dickerson, dressed now with his badge on and his belt full of bullets riding low under his belly. His deputies loomed behind him, but they weren't singing "Sweet Adeline."

"Okay, okay, break it up," he said, elbowing through the drifters. Then he came to Grandma.

"Dagnab it, Mrs. Dowdel, you're everywhere I turn. You're all over me like white on rice. *Now* what do you think you're doing?"

"I'm giving these boys the first eats they've had today."

"Or yesterday," a drifter said.

"Mrs. Dowdel, let me 'splain something to you," the sheriff bawled. "We don't want to feed these loafers. We want 'em out of town."

"They're out of town." Grandma pointed her spatula at

the sheriff's feet. "The town stops there. We're in the county."

"Yes, and I'm the sheriff of the county!" O. B. Dickerson bellowed. "You're in my jurisdiction!"

"Do tell," Grandma said. "Run me in."

The minute she said that, all the drifters looked up. That was when Sheriff Dickerson's deputies saw they were outnumbered.

"Mrs. Dowdel," the sheriff boomed, "I wouldn't know what to charge you with first. You're a one-woman crime wave. Where'd you get them fish, for instance?" he said, wisely overlooking the home brews in the drifters' hands.

"Out of a trap in Salt Crick," Grandma remarked. "Same as you get yours."

O. B. Dickerson's eyes bulged. "You accusing me, the sheriff of Piatt County, of running fish traps?" He poked his own chest with a pudgy finger.

"Not this morning," Grandma replied. "You was too drunk."

The drifters chuckled.

"And talkin' about this morning," the sheriff said, his face shading purple even in the darkness, "you stole my boat. That's what we call larceny, Mrs. Dowdel. You could go up for that."

"Oh well, the boat." Grandma made a little gesture with the spatula. "You'll find it tied up at Aunt Puss Chapman's dock. As a rule, I take it back where you tie it up. But of course I couldn't do that this morning. How could I row these grandkids of mine back past the Rod and Gun Club? They'd already seen what no child should—the sheriff and his deputies, blind drunk and naked as jaybirds, dancin' jigs on the porch and I don't know what all. It's like to have marked this girl for life."

Grandma nudged Mary Alice, who stood there in the big apron looking drooped and damaged.

"I'm thinkin' about taking her to the doctor so she can talk it out. I don't want her to develop one of them complexes you hear about."

"Whoa," the deputies murmured behind Sheriff Dickerson.

Earl T. Askew stepped up and said into his ear, "O.B., let's just let sleeping dogs lay. I got my hands full with Mrs. Askew as it is."

The sheriff simmered, but said, "Okay, Earl, if you say so." The sheriff and his posse were in retreat now. But he had to cover himself. "Mrs. Dowdel," he said, pulling a long face, "they's things I can overlook. But it seems to me you're runnin' a soup kitchen without a license from the Board of Health. I have an idea there's a law against that on the books."

"Go look it up, O.B.," Grandma said. "See if there's a law against feeding the hungry. But I have to tell you, you've talked so long, the evidence is all ate up."

And of course it was. The drifters had wolfed down the last morsel. With a small finger, Mary Alice pointed out the bare platters. Only a faint scent of fried catfish lingered on the night air. The empty beer bottles went without saying.

The drifters were moving off down the track, and the

deputies were heading back into town. O. B. Dickerson spit in the gravel, swung around, and followed them, his big boots grinding gravel.

We stacked the platters and rounded up the beer bottles for Grandma's next batch. I collapsed the legs on the card table. There wasn't a lot of music in Grandma, but she was humming as we worked, and I thought I recognized the tune:

> *The night that Paddy Murphy died*
> *I never shall forget. . . .*

Then after our quiet day in the country, we carried everything back across the road, under a silver-dollar moon.

The Day of Judgment

—⁓⁓—

1932

"I don't think Grandma's a very good influence on us," Mary Alice said. It had taken her a while to come to that conclusion, and I had to agree. It reconciled us some to our trips to visit her. Mary Alice was ten now. I believe this was the first year she didn't bring her jump rope with her. And she no longer pitched a fit because she couldn't take her best friends, Beverly and Audrey, to meet Grandma. "They wouldn't understand," Mary Alice said.

We weren't so sure Mother and Dad would either. Since we still dragged our heels about going, they didn't notice we looked forward to the trip.

The gooseberries were ripe when we got there that August. And come to find out, Grandma was famous for her gooseberry pies. Mary Alice and I were stemming berries at the kitchen table that first morning. Grandma was supervising a pan of them on the stove. The gooseberries popped softly as they burst open in boiling water.

Then somebody knocked on the front door. Grandma ran an arm across her forehead and started through the house. We'd have followed, but she said, "Keep at it."

When she came back, Mrs. L. J. Weidenbach, the banker's wife, was right behind her. If she'd thought she was going to be asked to sit down, she had another think coming. Grandma returned to the stove, leaving Mrs. Weidenbach beached by the kitchen table, where she overlooked Mary Alice and me.

She was big on top, though nowhere near as big as Grandma. But she had tiny feet, teetering in high-heeled shoes. The heat of the kitchen staggered her, but then people from Death Valley would have keeled over in Grandma's kitchen.

"Mrs. Dowdel, I am here on a mission," she said, "and I'll come right to the point."

"Do that," Grandma said.

"As you know, this is county fair week," Mrs. Weidenbach said, "the annual opportunity for our small community to make its mark."

Grandma said nothing.

"As you recall," Mrs. Weidenbach said, "my bread-and-butter pickles have taken the blue ribbon every year since the fair recommenced after the Great War."

If Grandma recalled this, she showed no sign.

"But my cucumbers this year haven't been up to snuff, not worth the brine for pickling. How were yours?"

"Didn't put any in," Grandma said.

"Ah well, you were wise." Mrs. Weidenbach's forehead began to look slick. It wasn't just the heat. "Mrs. Dowdel, I'll come clean. I don't think I better enter my bread-and-butter pickles this year, and I'm going to tell you why. The depression is upon us. Times are hard."

"They was never easy for me," Grandma recalled.

"And quite unfairly," Mrs. Weidenbach said, "people blame the bankers."

"My stars," Grandma said. "The bank forecloses on people's farms and throws them off their land, and they don't even appreciate it."

"Now, Mrs. Dowdel, don't be like that." Mrs. Weidenbach reached down the front of her dress and plucked up a lace handkerchief. She dabbed all around her mouth. "Mr. Weidenbach has asked me not to enter my bread-and-butter pickles into competition at the fair this year."

"Keep your head down till the depression blows over?"

"Something like that," Mrs. Weidenbach murmured. "So I naturally thought of you. After all, we've been neighbors these many years."

The Weidenbachs lived at the far end of town in the only brick house.

"I said to my husband, Mr. Weidenbach, somebody must carry home a blue ribbon to keep our town's name in front of the public. Otherwise, those county seat women will sweep the field. As you know, Mrs. Cowgill's decorative butter pats never do better than Honorable Mention."

If Grandma knew who won what at the county fair, she showed no sign.

"But there is nobody to touch you for baking with gooseberries. Even those of us who've never had a taste have heard. Word gets around."

"Try as a person will to keep it quiet," Grandma said.

"Gooseberries are tricky things," Mrs. Weidenbach went on. "Now, you take Mrs. Vottsmeier over at Bement. She wouldn't take on a gooseberry, but she'll pull down a blue ribbon in the Fruit Pies and Cobblers division with her individual cherry tarts if somebody doesn't put a stop to her."

Quiet followed as we listened to Grandma's wooden spoon scraping the sides of the stew pan. At length, she said, "I cook to eat, not to show off."

Mrs. Weidenbach sighed. "Mrs. Dowdel, these are desperate times. Don't hide your light under a bushel. It is up to you to hold high the banner for our town."

Grandma putting herself out for the fame of the town? I thought Mrs. Weidenbach was on the wrong track. On the other hand, Grandma liked to win.

Growing frantic, Mrs. Weidenbach let her gaze skim over Mary Alice and me. "And a day at the fair would be a nice outing for your grandkiddies."

"Wouldn't cut any ice with them," Grandma said. "They're from Chicago, so they've seen everything."

Instantly, an expression of great boredom fell over Mary Alice's face. I thought she might yawn. She was playing along with Grandma. I'd been thinking a day at the fair would be a welcome change, but I just shrugged and went on stemming gooseberries.

Grandma turned slightly from the stove. "Wouldn't have any way to get there if I wanted to go."

Mrs. Weidenbach brightened. "I will personally con-
duct you to the fair on prize day in my Hupmobile." She
waved a hand in benediction over us. "And there'll be
plenty of room for your grandkiddies."

"Oh well," Grandma said, "if I have an extra pie and
it's not raining that day . . ."

"Mrs. Dowdel, I knew you would stand and deliver!"
Mrs. Weidenbach clasped her hands. "And remember, even
the red ribbon for second prize will be better than
nothing."

Grandma gazed past her, seeming to count the corpses
on the flypaper strip. Mrs. Weidenbach was dismissed and
soon left. We all listened to the powerful roar as she
ground her Hupmobile into gear.

Grandma's sleeves were already turned back, or she'd
be turning them back now. She pointed at me. "Scoot
uptown and bring me a twenty-five-pound sack of sugar.
Tell them to stick it on my bill. After that I want every
gooseberry off them bushes out back." She turned on
Mary Alice. "And you're going to learn a thing or two
about pie crust."

There followed three of the busiest days of my young
life. Wrestling twenty-five pounds of sugar back from
Moore's Store was nothing to picking all the gooseberry
bushes clean. As Mrs. Weidenbach said, gooseberries are
tricky things—sour to the taste and spikey with stickers.
Not unlike Grandma. My throbbing hands were covered
with sticker wounds from getting all the gooseberries
into the pail. With towels around their middles and their
hair tucked up, Grandma and Mary Alice rolled out endless pastry on big breadboards.

We baked a gooseberry pie every four hours for the next three days. I had about all I could do to feed corncobs into the stove to keep the oven heat even. Gooseberries are so tart that more sugar than fruit goes into the pie. Some pies were still too sour, others gritty with too much sugar.

We tried and tried again. Grandma grew careful about balancing her ingredients, holding the measuring cup up to the light. She was like a scientist seeking the cure for something. I had to go back uptown for more sugar and another big can of Crisco. And we had to sample them all in search for the perfect pie. Mary Alice says she's never since been able to look a gooseberry in the face.

The day of judgment came. Mary Alice and I were in the parlor early, waiting. Grandma had told us to cover our heads against the fairground sun. I had on the Cubs cap I traveled in, and Mary Alice wore her straw from Easter. The house reeked of baking.

Then Grandma sailed like a galleon into the front room, striking us dumb. For her, dressing up usually meant taking off her apron. But this morning she wore a ready-made dress covered with flowers. The collar was fine net, fixed with a big cameo brooch that rode high. On her feet were large, unfamiliar shoes—white with the hint of a heel, and laces tied in big, perky bows. On her head was a hat with a big brim. The hatband on it happened to be a blue ribbon.

She glared, daring us to pay her a compliment. But the cat had our tongues. Mary Alice stared up at her, transfixed. Was she seeing herself fifty years hence?

66

The Hupmobile growled up outside, and the next thing you knew, we were in it. It wasn't as long as Al Capone's big Lincoln limousine, but it was the biggest car in this town. Mary Alice and I had the backseat to ourselves. The pie was in a box between my feet.

Grandma took charge of a small hamper full of our lunch, since they charge you two prices for everything at a fair. She rode up front beside Mrs. Weidenbach, with one big elbow propped outside the open window. The town had emptied out because this was prize day at the fair. But when we went by The Coffee Pot Cafe, there were faces at the window, and a loafer or two paused on the sidewalk to see us pass. Grandma inclined her head slightly. Most people wouldn't take their bows till after they'd won a blue ribbon, but Grandma wasn't most people.

The fairground was a pasture along a dusty road this side of the county seat. It was a collection of sheds and tents and a grandstand for the harness racing. But this was the big day for judging cattle, quilts, and cookery, so the grounds were packed, though it was a nickel to get in.

Mrs. Weidenbach twinkled along in her high heels next to Grandma. She didn't dare show her pickles, but she wanted some reflected glory in case the gooseberry pie won. "Let's run that pie over to the Domestic Sciences tent and get it registered," she said.

"I don't want it setting around," Grandma said. "The livestock draws flies." The pie was no burden to Grandma because I was carrying it. "Let's see something of the fair first," she said, managing to sound uninterested.

Along the midway the Anti-Horse-Thief Society had a stand selling burgoo and roasting ears. The 4-H club was offering chances on a heifer. Allis-Chalmers had a big tent showing their huskers and combines. Prohibition was about to be repealed, but the Temperance people had another big tent, offering ice water inside and a stage out front with a quartet performing. We stopped to hear them:

> You may drive your fast horse if you please,
> You may live in the very best style;
> Smoke the choicest cigars, at your ease,
> And may revel in pleasure awhile;
> Play billiards, from morning till night,
> Or loaf in the barroom all day,
> But just see if my words are not right:
> You will find, in the end, it don't pay.

At the other end of the midway was a rickety Ferris wheel, a merry-go-round, and a caterpillar. Beyond it was a sight that drew me. In an open stubblefield a biplane stood. Beside it was the pilot in a leather helmet with goggles, and puttees wrapped around his legs.

And a sign:

BARNSTORMING BARNIE BUCHANAN

AIR ACE

TRICK FLYING AND PASSENGER RIDES

My heart skipped a beat, and sank. Another sign read:

RIDES 75¢

I didn't have that kind of money on me. I didn't have any money on me. Still, my heart began to taxi. I'd never been in a plane, and my hero was Colonel Charles A. Lindbergh, who'd flown the Atlantic alone.

The American Legion was sponsoring Barnie Buchanan. A red-faced man in a Legionnaire's cap bawled through a megaphone, "Tell you what I'm going to do, folks. Any minute now Mr. Buchanan is going to show us his stuff by putting his machine through the same maneuvers he used in the Great War against the wily Hun. Then if you think six bits is still too steep, Mr. Buchanan has agreed to a special prize-day offer. To every blue ribbon winner, Mr. Buchanan will give a ride in his plane gratis. That's free of charge, ladies and gentlemen."

My heart left the ground, skimmed a hedgerow, and sailed into the wild blue yonder. The pie in my hands would win first prize since nobody but Grandma would take a chance with gooseberries. But she'd let me have her plane ride because she was too old and too big.

"You reckon that thing will get off the ground?" she said doubtfully, building my hopes higher.

"It looks like a box kite," Mary Alice said. "A person would have to be nuts to go up in it."

The biplane's wings were canvas-covered and much patched. It was more rickety than the Ferris wheel. Still, it was a plane, and this looked like my one chance in life to go up in one. Now Mrs. Weidenbach was plucking at Grandma's arm, and it was time to enter the pie into competition.

When we four went into the Domestic Sciences tent, Grandma remarked, "I said there'd be flies." Surrounded

by crowds, the long tables were all laid out: jams and pre-
serves, vegetables in novelty shapes, cakes and breads.
A half-sized cow carved out of butter reclined on a block
of melting ice. It was as hot as Grandma's kitchen in
the tent, so people fanned paper fans, compliments of
Broshear's Funeral Home, each with the Broshear motto
printed on it:

WHEN YOU COME TO THE END,
YOU'LL FIND A FRIEND

Mrs. Weidenbach averted her eyes as we passed Pickled
Products. I took charge of unpacking the pie and getting
it registered at Fruit Pies and Cobblers. Grandma started
at the other end of the table, casting an eye over the
competition. Everything looked good to me, and I was
wishing I was a judge so I could have a taste. A little card
with a number and a name stood beside each entry.

When she got to her own pie, Grandma froze. Next to
it was another lattice-topped gooseberry pie. There was
no doubt about it. Only gooseberries are that shade of
gray-green. And it was a very nice-looking pie. The edges
of its pastry were as neatly crimped as Grandma's. Maybe
better. She bent to read the card, and whipped around.

I followed her look as it fell on one of the smallest people in the tent. It was a man, one of the few there. A little
tiny man. He wore small bib overalls, a dress shirt, and a
bow tie. Four or five strands of hair were arranged across
his little bald head.

"Rupert Pennypacker," Grandma breathed. You seldom saw her caught off guard. Was he responsible for the other gooseberry pie?

"Who?" I said.

"The best home-baker in the state of Illinois," Grandma said. "Him and me come up together out in the country, so I know."

Mrs. Weidenbach quaked. Even Mary Alice looked concerned.

"I'm a goner," said Grandma.

A puttering sound deafened us. It was Barnie Buchanan, the air ace, right over our heads. He was doing his aerial stunts: barrel rolls and vertical figure eights, or whatever he did. Everybody looked up, though we could only see tent.

It was just a moment, but somehow I was sure. In that split second when we'd all looked up, I thought Grandma had switched her pie's card with Rupert Pennypacker's. It was a desperate act, but as Mrs. Weidenbach had said, these were desperate times. It was the wrong thing for Grandma to do, but I might get a plane ride out of it. My head swam.

Grandma nudged me away from the table and elbowed through a parting crowd. She was making for Mr. Pennypacker. I wondered if she'd reach down, grab him by his bib, and fling him out of the tent. With Grandma, you never knew. "Rupert," she said.

Standing beside him was the scariest-looking old lady I'd ever seen, weirder than Aunt Puss Chapman. She was only a little taller than Mr. Pennypacker and dressed all in black, including the veil on her hat. She had warts, and her chin met her hat brim. There was a lump in her cheek that looked like it might be a bunch of chaw.

"You remember Mama," Mr. Pennypacker said to Grandma.

His voice was high, like it had never changed. My voice hadn't changed either, but I was twelve, so I still had hope.

His old mama hissed something in his ear and tried to pull him away with a claw on his arm.

"Well, may the best man win," Grandma said, turning on her heel. By now the judges were at work. They carried little silver knives and miniature trowels for sampling the cobblers and pies. Tension mounted.

Nervously, Mrs. Weidenbach said to Grandma, "What a nice, moist consistency your pie filling has, Mrs. Dowdel. I'm sure it will be noted. How much water did you add to the mixture?"

"About a mouthful," Grandma replied.

The judging went on forever, but nobody left the sweltering tent. We all watched the judges chewing. Finally, Mary Alice said she thought she might faint, so I took her outside.

Up among the clouds Barnie Buchanan was still putting his old biplane through its paces. He dived to earth, then pulled up in time. He gave us three loops and a snap roll. And my heart was up there with him, scouting for Germans.

A voice rose from inside the tent, followed by gusts of applause. They were announcing the winners: honorable mention, third prize, second—first. I didn't want to go back in there. I hoped we'd win, but I wasn't sure we should. Not if Grandma had switched—

The tent quivered with one final burst of applause. People began streaming out, flowing around us. Then out strolled Mr. Pennypacker and his mama, clutching him. You couldn't read anything in that face of hers, but Mr. Pennypacker was beaming. From the clasp on his overall bib hung a blue ribbon.

"Shoot," Mary Alice said. "After all that pie crust I rolled out." In a way I was relieved. But then I saw my one and only chance for a plane ride crash and burn. Mr. Pennypacker was already heading for the field where the biplane was coming in for a landing.

At last Mrs. Weidenbach and Grandma came out. A nod from Grandma sent me back to the Hupmobile for our hamper of lunch. We ate it at a table in the Temperance tent, sliced chicken washed down with ice water. Grandma had her great stone face on, but Mrs. Weidenbach tried to make the best of things.

"Never mind, Mrs. Dowdel. As I have said, a red ribbon for second place is not to be sneezed at or scorned. You did right well."

But Grandma hadn't come to the fair for second prize. She didn't wear it, if she'd bothered to collect it at all. "And you were up against stiff competition," Mrs. Weidenbach said. "I daresay Rupert Pennypacker has had nothing to do all his life but wait on his dreadful mother and bake."

Consoling Grandma was a thankless task. She ate her chicken sandwich with her usual appetite, observing the crowds. If I could read her mind at all, she was thinking she could do with a cold beer.

The day seemed to have peaked and was going downhill now. As we left the Temperance tent, the quartet was singing, in close harmony:

> . . . *Lips that touch wine*
> *Will never touch mine.* . . .

We were ready to head for the parking pasture, but Grandma turned us the other way, toward the midway and the biplane.

"Wha—" said Mrs. Weidenbach, but fell silent.

We were walking through the fair, and something inside my rib cage began to stir. There ahead, the biplane was on the ground. Afternoon sun played off the dull mahogany of its propeller. Something within me dared to dream. I wasn't swooping. I didn't even taxi, but I was walking lighter.

Giving blue ribbon winners free rides hadn't stimulated much business. Barnie Buchanan was lounging beside his plane. He was smoking another cigarette in a cupped hand, pilot-style.

Grandma strode past the ticket table, out onto the field. She paused to look the plane over from prop to tail. Then she glanced briefly down at me. I didn't dare look up at her. But my hopes were rising. Then she marched forward. When Barnie Buchanan saw Grandma bearing down on him, he tossed away his cigarette.

"I'm a blue ribbon winner," Grandma announced, "here for my ride."

"Wha—" Mrs. Weidenbach said.

My brain went dead.

"Well, ma'am," Barnie Buchanan said uncertainly, noticing her size. "And what class did you compete in?"

"Fruit Pies and Cobblers." She held up a crumpled blue ribbon clutched in her fist. She gave him a glimpse of it, then dropped the ribbon into her pocketbook.

"Well, ma'am, it seems to me I've already given a ride to a man who won first in pies," he said. "A little fellow."

"Oh that's Rupert Pennypacker," Grandma said. "You got that turned around in your mind. He won in Sausage and Headcheese. Don't I look more like a pie baker than him?"

Grandma reached up to pull the pin out of her hat. She handed the hat to Mary Alice. "Here, hold this. It might blow off." I saw the hatband was missing from her hat, the blue ribbon.

It took three big members of the American Legion and Barnie Buchanan to get Grandma into the front cockpit of the plane. Eventually, the sight drew a crowd. The Legionnaires would invite Grandma to step into their clasped hands, then boost her up. That didn't work.

Then they'd hoist her up some other way, but she'd get halfway there, and her hindquarters would be higher than her head. They had an awful job getting her into the plane, and they were wringing wet. But at last she slid into the seat, to a round of applause from the crowd. Grandma was a tight fit, and the plane seemed to bend beneath her. Barnie Buchanan stroked his chin. But then he pulled his goggles over his eyes and sprang up to the rear seat. He could pilot the plane from there, if he could see around Grandma. A Legionnaire jerked the propeller and the motor coughed twice, then roared.

Mrs. Weidenbach was between Mary Alice and me now, clutching our hands.

A lot of Grandma stuck up above the plane. The breeze stirred her white hair, loosening the bun on the back. Her spectacle lenses flashed like goggles. She raised one hand in farewell, and the plane began to bump down the field.

Now my heart was in my mouth. Everyone's was. The biplane, heavy-burdened, lumbered over uneven ground, trying to gather speed. It drew nearer and nearer the hedgerow at the far end of the field.

"Lift!" the crowd cried. "Lift!" Mary Alice's hands were over her eyes.

But then distant dust spurted from the plane's front wheels. The tail rose, but dropped down again. It had stopped just short of the hedgerow, and now it was turning back. We watched the bright disc of the whirling propeller as the biplane returned to us.

Barnie Buchanan dropped down from the cockpit. He looked pale, shaken. Boy, did he need a cigarette. But they had to get Grandma down from the plane, and getting her out was twice the job of getting her in. She'd plant one big shoe on a shoulder and the other on another. They had her by the ankles, then by the hips. She tipped forward and back, and the pocketbook swinging from her arm pummeled their heads. She brought two big men to their knees.

At last she was on solid ground, scanning the crowd for me. She crooked a finger, and I went forth. As always, I couldn't see a moment ahead.

"Ma'am, I'm sorry," Barnie Buchanan was saying to Grandma. "But I was just carrying a little more . . . freight than this old crate could handle."

Grandma waved that away. "Don't give it a thought. You can take my grandson instead," she said. "If he wants to go."

The heavens opened. I thought I heard celestial music. Somehow I was up in the front seat of the plane, buckling myself in with trembling hands. And Barnie Buchanan was handing me up a pair of goggles. Goggles from the Great War.

Now we were taxiing, Barnie and me, bumping over the ground, gathering speed behind the yearning motor. And I felt that moment when we left the ground, and the fair fell away below us, and ahead of us was nothing but the towering white clouds. And beyond them sky, endless sky. I didn't know there was that much sky, as we flew, Barnie and me, in stuttering circles higher than birds, over the patchwork fields.

That night Mary Alice went up to bed early, tuckered out. Still in her fair finery, Grandma sat in the platform rocker, working out of her shoes. They'd been a torment to her all day. Now she kicked them aside. "If I could pop all the corns on my toes," she said, "I could feed a famine."

I'd settled on the settee, watching her in the circle of light, after the big doings of the day.

"Grandma," I said at last. "I've got a couple of things on my mind."

"Well, spit 'em out," she said, "if you must."

"About your plane ride. You never did expect it to get off the ground, did you?"

"Lands no." She turned down a hand. "When I was dainty enough for a plane to lift, they didn't have them. We couldn't have dusted the crops with me on board. I just wanted to see what it felt like sitting up there in that hen roost."

"Cockpit, Grandma," I said. "Then you meant for me to have the ride all along?"

Grandma didn't reply.

"And another thing. I've got a confession to make," I said. "I know you wanted first prize on the pie. You wanted it bad. And I thought you'd switched the card on Mr. Pennypacker's pie with yours so you could win with his pie."

She shot me her sternest look. But then easing back in the platform rocker, she said, "I did."

The Phantom Brakeman

1933

Down at Grandma's the only thing that reminded us of home and Chicago was Nehi. This was orange pop at a nickel a bottle. With the twenty-five cents apiece that Dad gave Mary Alice and me, we could each buy five Nehis during our week, if we could slip off from Grandma long enough to get our allowances spent.

The Coffee Pot Cafe kept the Nehis along with the Grapettes and the Dr Peppers in a sheet-metal vat of ice water with a bottle opener hanging down on a piece of twine. Grandma said she didn't like Nehi because the bubbles in it gave her gas. Mary Alice said anything that cost money gave Grandma gas.

We made ourselves scarce that first afternoon and headed

uptown before Grandma could find us some chores. I was thirteen at last, so I'd thank you to call me Joe, not Joey, and I walked a few strides ahead of Mary Alice.

For one thing, she'd been taking dancing lessons all year and never went anywhere without her tap shoes in a drawstring bag. The greatest movie star in history was sweeping the country at that time, a girl younger than Mary Alice named Shirley Temple. Shirley could sing and act, and she was a tap-dancing demon. Every girl in America was taking tap to be the next Shirley Temple.

Though Mary Alice was getting a little too leggy to be a child star, Mother said taking tap would give her poise. So Mary Alice was apt to stop cold on a sidewalk and run through a tap routine in her regular sandals. I wasn't going to wait while she did that, so we each acted like the other one wasn't there.

The only people in The Coffee Pot were a couple of farm women passing the time of day with Mrs. Ike Cripe. As proprietor, Mrs. Cripe wore a crocheted handkerchief pinned to her apron, and a hair net. She saw us come in. First the screen door closed behind me. Then it opened again, and Mary Alice made her entrance. You could tell that Mrs. Cripe wanted our nickels before we fished the Nehis out of the water. She was deep in conversation with the farm women, but when I started to put my nickel on the counter, her palm was outstretched to take it.

Above on the wall was a framed picture of Franklin Delano Roosevelt, who'd beaten out Hoover as president of the United States. He hung between two signs:

DOUBLE-YOLK BREAKFAST
SERVED ALL DAY
with sausage, bacon, or ham, your choice
20¢

and

BLUE PLATE SPECIAL
liverwurst or tuna sandwich
cup of our coffee thrown in
10¢

Mrs. Cripe and the farm women were remarking on what a handsome man Franklin Delano Roosevelt was.

"Don't it beat all how a man that good-lookin' would marry a wife that plain?" said one of the farm women, who'd have known a thing or two about plainness. "That Mrs. Eleanor Roosevelt is plain as a mud fence."

"Maybe she's a good cook," the other farm woman offered. "Kissin' don't last. Good cookin' does."

Mrs. Cripe rang up two nickel sales on the register. "Men don't have any idea about women," she said. This big statement quieted the farm women. Then Mrs. Cripe said, "They's cousins, you know."

"Who is?"

"The Roosevelts. He married his cousin."

The toothpicks stopped dead in the farm women's mouths. "You don't mean it."

"It was in the paper." Mrs. Cripe reached under her apron to adjust a strap.

"Was it legal?" a farm woman whispered.

"I couldn't say," Mrs. Cripe replied. "Them Roosevelts isn't Illinois people."

Their voices dropped lower. I'd noticed before, marrying your cousin was a touchy subject around here. But now it was time for our Nehis. Half the pleasure was sticking your arm in up to the shirtsleeve and fishing in the ice water for the bottle.

Mary Alice plunged in at her end. We took our time. In those days before air-conditioning, just getting one arm cooled off was a treat. We elbowed aside the Grapettes. You didn't get enough for your money with a Grapette, and it left your mouth purple. And the Dr Peppers tasted like cough medicine. When we had our Nehis in hand and opened, Mary Alice took a booth at the back. I settled at the table with the checkerboard in the front window.

In the past Mrs. Cripe had a fry cook and another lady working the counter. But she was down to herself now, except for a girl who was wiping the tables with a wet rag. You had to look twice to see her. She was that skinny, and pale as a ghost. A light breeze would have blown her into the back room. But she was keeping busy. She went at the tabletops like she was killing rats.

When she worked her way to Mary Alice's booth, they fell into a murmuring conversation. Mary Alice took out her tap shoes to show her, so it must be girl talk. I was glad to be up here away from it. I was coming to the age when I didn't know how near girls I was supposed to be.

Mrs. Cripe didn't ring up a sale after the farm women left, so they may have come in just for the toothpicks. I was making my Nehi last. Then from my seat in the window I saw a woman pull up out front. She dropped down from a buckboard and tied her old mule to the rail. The mule wore a straw hat, and the woman wore a sunbonnet. She was the toughest-looking woman you ever saw. She made Mrs. Ike Cripe look like a movie star.

Stomping through the front door in a pair of unmatching shoes, she made for the cash register. For a bad moment I thought she was going to hold up the place.

"Well, Miz Eubanks," Mrs. Cripe said, "what is it?"

The sunbonnet woman, Miz Eubanks, stuck a grubby paw under Mrs. Cripe's nose. "Let me have my girl's wages." She jerked her head to the back booth where the wispy girl was lingering at Mary Alice's table.

"I give her her fifteen cents already today," Mrs. Cripe said.

"You done paid her before she worked out her day?" Miz Eubanks was confounded. "A fool and her money is soon parted." She headed for the wispy girl, whose eyes looked hunted and scared.

Grabbing the front of the girl's uniform, she said, "Gimme that fifteen cents, or I'll turn you every way but loose."

The girl hung there in her mother's grasp. Mary Alice sat below them, stunned. In a small voice the girl said, "I need my money."

"You don't have no needs, except I say so," the woman barked, nose to nose with her. "Cough it up."

When she turned her loose, the girl reached down as slow as she dared and took something out of her shoe. It must have been the full fifteen cents because Miz

Eubanks's hand closed over it, making a fist. She shook it at the girl.

"And when you get home tonight, I'll take your back wages out of your hide. Girl, you won't set down till the first frost. I know what you're up to, missy. You're sly, but you don't put nothin' over on me."

She stalked out of the place, past Mrs. Cripe, who hadn't liked being called a fool. The girl stood beside Mary Alice, trying not to cry.

Mary Alice reached up to touch her hand. She was trying to say something to make the girl feel better. But I didn't look or listen. I didn't know what to do.

Pretty soon we started for home. I'd left some Nehi in the bottom of the bottle, and I think Mary Alice did too. We walked together now. I waited when she stopped on an unbroken slab of sidewalk and went into one of her tap steps. She held her skirts out in the Shirley Temple way, but her heart wasn't in it. She was just going through the motions, and her mind was somewhere else.

"Who was that girl anyway?" I said finally.

"Vandalia Eubanks," she said, "and that old crow in the bonnet was her mother. She wants to rule Vandalia's life."

I shrugged. "Well, she's her mother."

"She's her *jailer*," Mary Alice said. "Vandalia's *seventeen*."

"Seventeen? She doesn't look twelve."

"A starved seventeen," Mary Alice said. "And she needs a friend." Then her jaw clamped shut in Grandma's own way, and she didn't say anything else all the way home.

When we got there, Grandma was out in the yard, standing over a thing made out of lumber in the shape of a teepee. Nearby was a pile of stove lengths on the circle of burned ground where she cooked down her apples for apple butter.

She waved us over. "We're makin' soap."

Until we started coming to Grandma's, we thought soap was a pink bar that came out of a wrapper labeled *Cashmere Bouquet*. But that cost seven cents, and Grandma made her own. She soon had us busy as bird dogs. She sent Mary Alice to the pump for pail after pail of water, and she sent me to the house for coal scuttles full of wood ash from the kitchen stove. Grandma poured the water through the teepee, which was a hopper. When it dropped through the ash, it came out as lye. Grandma caught it in a pan. We worked till supper time. Before we went inside, she built up a big fire from the stove lengths and shavings.

After supper Grandma and I worked through what she called the cool of the evening. Mary Alice had managed to vanish, but the heavy work was over. The fire had burned down just right. Over the glowing embers Grandma put an old pot on a tripod. We'd dumped the lye into it, with just the right amount of water. Now she added what looked to me like garbage. Ham skins, bacon rinds, and things too mysterious to mention.

We took turns stirring this witches' brew as darkness crawled across the yard. The blossoms on the morning glory vine were little tight blue fists, and you could hear husky sighing from the cornfield across the fence.

Grandma looked up—far out to the west, down where the road and the Wabash tracks seemed to meet. She scanned the far horizon, maybe waiting for me to ask what she was looking for.

"What are you looking for, Grandma?"

"The brakeman," she said, still scanning.

"You mean a brakeman off the Wabash Railroad?"

She nodded. "This is about the time of evening he's been known to show."

"Who is he, Grandma?"

She turned on me. "You mean you never heard the story?" She took over the stirring, turning the paddle with both hands. "It happened back in 1871. And it all come to pass because of the Great Fire of Chicago. The town of Decatur was sending a special train full of volunteers up to fight that fire Mrs. O'Leary's cow started.

"Of course, railroad signals was very simple in them early times. And it was a foggy night. Somehow, the train full of firefighters got on the same track as a Wabash freight train. They met head on. It was just a half mile along them tracks, down by that stand of timber on the way to Salt Crick."

Grandma nodded down the road to the timber, a dark smudge in the distance.

"Killed a brakeman on the freight train and both engineers. Oh, you never saw such a mess." Grandma shook her head. "I was only a babe in arms, but I remember it well. My maw walked the tracks down there and held me up to see it. They'd pried the locomotives apart and taken out the dead. But it was a sight to behold. They said the dead bodies looked like they'd been fed through a sausage grinder."

I swallowed hard, but I was always interested in anything from her early life that might explain Grandma.

The paddle in her hand turned slow in the foul brew as she looked down to the dark woods. "Unfortunately, that wasn't the end of the story." She glanced my way. "The brakeman's been seen since."

The darkness deepened around us, and a star or two came out. "The brakeman who got chewed up like he'd been through a sausage grinder?"

Grandma nodded. "Years go by without a sighting. Then on a hazy night somebody'll see the brakeman down there between the rails, swinging an old-time railroad lantern. Or they'll spot a dim yellow light deep in the timber, like he's a wandering soul, still trying to head off the oncoming train."

"Grandma," I said in a breaking voice, though my voice was beginning to break anyway, "are you talking about the brakeman's ghost?"

She pursed her lips to give a considered opinion. "I don't say one way or the other. All I know is some people won't go down that road after dark by theirselves."

Grandma had hiked her skirts to keep them out of the fire, and the glowing embers made it hot as noon. But goose bumps popped out on my arms.

"Of course, I'm talkin' about ignorant people," Grandma said. "Superstitious people."

I had some trouble settling down that night. It was the first night of the visit, so that was normal. But every time my eyes closed, I saw the phantom brakeman with hamburger meat for a face, swinging a ghostly lantern through tree branches like skeletons.

So I was up and down. As bad luck would have it, my bedroom window looked west to the haunted woods. I'd keep getting up to look in case a lantern was swinging in the trees. But I didn't see anything.

Then I was no sooner asleep than I was awake again. Some sound woke me. I didn't move in the bed, hoping not to hear any more. But I heard some snuffling, like crying. It seemed to come from Mary Alice's room. I thought I heard her voice too, just a few words, though she never talked in her sleep.

Now I was bolt awake, and the goose bumps were back. Wearing only my BVDs, I got up and looked out in the hall. Mary Alice's door was shut tight, though we never closed our bedroom doors, hoping for a breeze. I crept over, but didn't try the knob, which was bound to be locked. I rapped lightly. This brought forth a little startled yipping sound from inside.

Quicker than if I'd awakened her, little feet padded across her creaking floor. Her keyhole spoke. "What?"

"Mary Alice, are you alone in there?"

"Who wants to know?"

"Who do you think? Are you?"

". . . No," she said. "And don't whisper so loud."

"Who's in there with you?"

"A puppy."

"A *puppy?*" I said. "Where'd you get a puppy?"

"The cobhouse."

"You don't go in the cobhouse," I said.

"He came out. He followed me home. I'm calling him Skipper. That's what you're hearing, Joey. Don't tell Grandma. She doesn't believe in indoor pets."

88

I gave up, though I didn't quite believe in the pet either, Skipper or whoever. But I was too tired to argue. I went back to bed and slept like a log.

Grandma had already eaten her breakfast. She was at the stove, fixing ours. Sausage patties, which reminded me of the brakeman. And buttermilk biscuits and fried eggs over easy. Mary Alice turned up promptly, looking perky and innocent. I remembered Skipper.

When Grandma's back was turned, Mary Alice broke open a biscuit and stuck a sausage patty inside it. Then she pushed it down her shirt. She knew I was watching, but she didn't meet my eye. The eggs were runny, so that was a problem for her. She thought about making an egg sandwich to go with the other biscuit, but gave it up. When Grandma turned back to the table, Mary Alice had licked her platter clean. She skidded out of her chair and was gone, back upstairs. Grandma gave her departing figure a long look.

She'd mentioned that the night air would cool her brew to soap, so we went outside to see. The embers were white, and sure enough, the pot was solid with soap. Something like soap.

It reminded me of the cheese she fed the catfish, and it didn't smell much better. My job was to pry it out of the pot. Grandma hunkered in the grass with a butcher knife to carve it into cakes.

"This here's good soap," she remarked as she went at it with the knife. "It lathers good, and it'll take the top layer of skin right off you."

The sun hadn't been up long, and the morning glories

were just beginning to unfurl. Then far down the road a cloud of dust appeared, heading for town. Nearer, it was Miz Eubanks, the strings on her sunbonnet flying. She was standing up in her buckboard with a whip in her hand. Her old straw-hatted mule was galloping. I'd never seen a mule break into a trot, let alone a full gallop.

The buckboard sped past the house, never slowing for town. Grandma stood up to watch it pass, fingering her chins thoughtfully.

She gave me the chore of scraping out the soap pot, which looked like a long day's work. I had to roll the pot in the grass and climb halfway in with a wire brush to loosen the clinging soap. It was a mean job, and some very strange-smelling stuff had gone into that soap. Grandma'd said that the full recipe for it would die with her.

In an hour's time I hadn't made a dent in it. By then Mary Alice had come out on the back porch, wearing her tap shoes. She began to run through one of her routines, calling out the steps:

> *Shuffle, ball, change, step, step*
> *Shuffle, ball, change, step, step*

I was scraping away on the pot, and she was tapping away on the porch, and if you asked me, she was acting entirely too innocent.

We heard a clopping of hooves and a jangle of harness, and here came Miz Eubanks in her buckboard, back from uptown. She swerved into Grandma's side yard and drew up. The old mule was foaming at the mouth and looked near death. Its straw hat was hanging from an ear.

Miz Eubanks dropped down and lit running. She pounded up on the back porch, shoving Mary Alice aside. But even Miz Eubanks didn't quite dare to storm into Grandma's house. She gave the screen door a savage rattle though.

Grandma appeared, big behind screen wire. "Well, Idella," she said, "what have you got a burr under your tail about now?"

Miz Eubanks was wheezing. She turned up the sleeves on her feedsack dress. "I need my girl back. You've got her in there."

"What have I got that's yours?" Grandma queried.

"Vandalia. You've got her. She didn't come home last night, and she ain't at work today. She was seen comin' in this house. That girl done brought her." Miz Eubanks poked a finger in Mary Alice's face, which was frozen with fear.

I was observing the scene over the rim of the soap pot, and I was all eyes.

"Who seen her come in here?" Grandma said. "I didn't."

"Everybody in town," Miz Eubanks barked.

Grandma nodded. She knew everybody knew everything, often before it happened.

"Well, let me tell you how it'll be, Idella," Grandma said in a reasonable voice. "If you want to search my house, you'll have to get past me. And I'll tell you something else for free. If you set a foot over that doorsill, I'll wring your red neck."

Miz Eubanks made one of her fists and seemed about to put it through the screen door. She was dancing with rage. With a strangled cry, she dashed off the porch, heading for the buckboard. Her old mule saw her coming and shied.

She rattled off the property, and Mary Alice stood there on the porch, wilting.

Things quieted down after that. Grandma disappeared from the screen door. I went back to scraping the pot, and pretty soon Mary Alice went back to practicing her tap. But real slow. Her timing was all off.

By noon I knocked off work for a stop at the privy before dinner. I was almost in it with only one thing on my mind when something moved in the cobhouse door. Somebody was there, and he stepped out into my path. I nearly jumped over the privy.

It was a guy in a tight suit, a high collar, and a silk necktie. I'd seen him uptown, but couldn't put a name to him. He looked me over and decided I was old enough that he'd have to deal with me.

"Junior Stubbs," he said, putting out a hand to shake.

"Ah," I said. "Could you wait a minute?"

When I came out of the privy, he gave me a business card that read:

STUBBS & ASKEW

General Insurance Agents
Wind and Fire Coverage Our Specialty

"I'm in business with my daddy," he explained. "Merle Stubbs."

I fingered the card. "I doubt if my grandma is in the market for any insurance."

"Mrs. Dowdel?" he said. "Oh no. You can't sell her anything."

He had a jiggly Adam's apple, I noticed. "I happened to be passing," he said.

"Between the cobhouse and the privy?"

"Well, no." He looked down at his shoes. "I was holed up here, to tell you the truth. I'm on my lunch hour. You got Vandalia Eubanks in your house, am I right?"

"Everybody says so," I said. "Why? Do you want to sell Vandalia some insurance?"

"No," he said. "I want *her*."

I blinked in the midday sun while he waited for me to work this out. "Could you get a message to Vandalia?" he asked, pulling out another of his cards. "You can read what's on the back of it, just to show you I mean business."

I turned the card over and read,

Come steal away with me, sweetheart,
Let nothing no longer keep us apart,
Break yourself free of your mother's rule,
She never knew love and she's just being cruel.
I love you, honey,

Junior

My ears burned like fire. Now that I was thirteen, it took less than this to embarrass me.

"Do your best," he said. "It's now or never for me. If her old ma gets her home again, I'm a dead duck. Tell Vandalia I'll be back in the cobhouse tonight by dark, with hope in my heart."

Then Junior cut out. I watched him scale Grandma's back fence in his suit.

By midafternoon I'd done all I could do on the soap pot, and a nickel was burning a hole in my pocket. I was thinking hard about a Nehi. But before I could make my escape, a car pulled up in front of Grandma's house, a 1930 Ford Model A sedan. A lady and a man got out and started up the front walk. I went in the kitchen door, not wanting to miss anything.

Grandma was already at the front door, and Mary Alice was hanging around the foot of the stairs that led up to the bedrooms. I palmed Junior's poem to her, and she stuck it down the front of her shirt where the sausage sandwich had earlier gone.

"Junior'll be in the cobhouse by nightfall," I murmured. And Mary Alice nodded.

"Whatever you're selling, Merle," Grandma was saying at the front door, "I don't want any."

Mr. Merle Stubbs and his wife overflowed the front door. "Now, Mrs. Dowdel, I'm not here in my professional capacity. I have took time off work and brought Mrs. Stubbs with me to have a friendly word with you."

They got their feet in the door, and Grandma let them take chairs in the front room. "What do you want?" she said, not sitting.

"Nothing in the world but to chat with you on a private matter." Mr. Stubbs shifted one leg over the other.

"There's no private matters in this town, Merle," Grandma said. "Everybody's private business is public property."

"Yes, and you've stuck your nose in ours!" Mrs. Stubbs said, speaking up sharp. "You got that Eubanks gal upstairs this minute." Mrs. Stubbs glared at the ceiling. "She's trying to steal my son, and you're helping her out. She's gotten away from her maw, so she's halfway there!"

Grandma's spectacles flashed her a warning. But Mr. Stubbs said, "Now, now, Mrs. Stubbs is upset and off her feed about our boy, Junior. He's lost all his judgment and wants to marry a Eubanks."

"Do tell." Grandma's big arms were folded in front of her. "So what?"

"We've got a position in the community," Mr. Stubbs said. "We don't need a connection with such as the Eubankses. I'm as democratic as the next guy, but there's limits. Besides, Idella Eubanks is half-cracked, and it could run in the family. Think of the children."

"Have you talked it over with Junior?" Grandma asked.

"You can't talk sense to him," Mrs. Stubbs replied. "He's bewitched."

Mary Alice and I lurked near, taking in every word. About the only thing Vandalia and Junior had going for them as a couple was that they weren't cousins.

A thud occurred then. Mary Alice and I both heard it. Something hit the outside of the house, nothing loud. Just a thud. Grandma heard. She began to drift toward the front door, but she went on talking to the Stubbses. "Well, it's no skin off my nose," she said calmly, "but seems like your boy's old enough to make up his own mind. How old is he?"

"Thirty," Mrs. Stubbs said, "but he's a young thirty."

Grandma was at the front door now. She pulled it open and stalked outside. We all followed, naturally, to find her in the middle of the yard with her hands on her hips, staring back at the house.

A ladder had appeared, propped against the sill of an upstairs bedroom window. On the top of the ladder was Miz Idella Eubanks in her sunbonnet. She was working away, trying to jimmy loose the catch on a window screen.

Grandma gazed. Of all the invasions of her privacy, this one took the cake.

"For the love of Pete!" Mrs. Stubbs looked up, shading her eyes. "It's that trashy Eubanks woman trying to get her girl back. I hope she does! I hope she takes her home and sticks her down the well!"

Miz Eubanks had to notice the yard below had filled up with people. But now she had the screen loose and was ducking under to get inside. She had one knee on the sill.

That's as far as she got. Grandma strolled over and took the ladder in both hands. She jerked it free of the ground, and it fell, scraping down the house.

It must have seemed to Miz Eubanks that the world had dropped out from under her. She had one knee on the windowsill and the rest of her was in space. She grabbed the window screen, and it came with her as she fell.

She was in the air a long moment, turning as she dropped, legs working hard. Then she crashed through the snowball bushes, still clutching the screen.

"Jumping Jehoshaphat!" Mr. Stubbs cried, "and she's not insured!"

The top of a nodding snowball had snagged her sunbonnet, but Miz Eubanks herself was down among the roots, beginning to crawl out from under the bushes that had broken her fall. Again she was wheezing.

Forgetting their differences, Mr. Stubbs would have gone to her aid. But Mrs. Stubbs took him in hand and headed to their Ford. Over her shoulder Mrs. Stubbs called back, "I hope this puts an end to the entire unfortunate business. And I don't want any more interference from you, Mrs. Dowdel!"

"Get in the car, Lula," Mr. Stubbs said. And they gunned away as fast as a Ford goes.

Miz Eubanks sat in the yard, dazed. Grandma stood above her. "There's my property line," she said, pointing it out. "Get over it."

Miz Eubanks limped away, steaming. Where she'd parked her mule I didn't know, if it was still alive. She turned around just off Grandma's territory. "You done abdicated my girl," she howled, "but I'll git her back. You watch!"

I looked up at the bedroom window with the missing screen. A face appeared there briefly, ghostly pale. And it wasn't Skipper the puppy.

By eight o'clock that night the whole town knew everything. Defying his parents, Lula and Merle, Junior Stubbs was known to be in Grandma's cobhouse, waiting to make his move. And Vandalia Eubanks, tucked away upstairs in Grandma's house, was ready to make hers, in spite of her half-cracked mother, Idella.

The Wabash Cannonball train was due through on its run between Detroit and St. Louis. It was going to make its usual quick stop at 8:17, and the runaway couple were going to elope on it. Everybody said so.

The Coffee Pot Cafe was doing its best business in several years because its front windows looked out on the depot. Word had spread, and people had driven in from all over the county to witness the showdown. The Stubbses meant to be on the platform to talk Junior out of it. The whole Eubanks clan was coming to town to get Vandalia back. Nobody agreed on how many big brothers she had, but there were several.

Things didn't go according to plan, though. When the Wabash Cannonball steamed in on schedule, the town bulged with people, but the lovebirds, Junior and Vandalia, were absent.

The Cannonball pulled out without them, leaving Merle and Lula Stubbs and all the Eubankses milling on the platform. The train gathered speed past Grandma's house, and Grandma was at the front door to see it go through. Mary Alice watched from an upstairs bedroom window.

But then with a piercing shriek that rent the evening air, the powerful locomotive set its brakes. It skidded a quarter of a mile before it could come to a stop.

There was a little haze that night, a little mist. Down by the haunted timber a deathly figure stood, shrouded in black, swinging an old-time lantern. The Phantom Brakeman seemed to hover between the tracks, dimly bathed in yellow lantern light. The engineer stuck his head out of the locomotive and stared down the track with widening eyes. Before he could send the fireman to investigate, the ghastly figure had vanished in the haze, melted in the mist.

But it gave Vandalia and Junior their chance. They came up, hand in hand, from the other side of the Wabash tracks and scrambled aboard the open platform at the back of the parlor car. When the Cannonball pulled out again, they were on it, together at last.

That was one night Grandma didn't have to wake herself up to go to bed. As I came in the front room, she was there in her platform rocker, saying to Mary Alice, "Next time you bring a stray home, make it a puppy."

Mary Alice stared.

"You can call it Skipper," Grandma suggested.

"How'd you know—"

"I heard you tell your brother that Vandalia Eubanks was a puppy. I can hear all over the house. I got ears on me like an Indian scout. And I don't sleep."

Grandma looked up at me. "Get everything squared away?" she asked.

And yes, I had. I'd taken off Grandpa Dowdel's big old black overcoat and put it back in the cobhouse with the old lantern, where I'd found them.

Things with Wings

—⟡—

1934

When we got down off the train, Grandma was there on the platform. After our first visit she'd never met us at the train, figuring we could find our own way. But here she was, under her webby old black umbrella to shade her from the sun.

But she wasn't there to meet us. She was seeing somebody off. A lady was climbing up into the car behind ours. We caught only a squint in the dazzling light, but knew the hat. It was Mrs. Effie Wilcox. With a powerful arm, Grandma swung Mrs. Wilcox's bulging valise aboard, then a picnic hamper. She stepped back as the Blue Bird pulled out. She didn't wave, but scanned the windows to see if Mrs. Wilcox found a seat. Then Grandma turned to us.

You could never call her a welcoming woman, but today her mind was truly miles away. I was falling behind with our suitcase, though this year I was nearly as tall as Grandma herself.

"Was Mrs. Wilcox going on a trip?" Mary Alice inquired.

"She's gone for good," Grandma said. "Off to double up with her sister at Palmyra. Bank's foreclosing on her house, so she lit out, not wanting to watch them dump her stuff in the road. After Wilcox died, she left the farm and bought that house in town. But she can't keep up with the payments."

At noon dinner that day Mary Alice and I distracted Grandma with all the excitement we'd left behind in Chicago. In July they'd killed John Dillinger, Public Enemy Number One. He'd been on a long spree, robbing banks throughout the middle west. The public didn't know whether they wanted him caught or not. He'd provided a lot of entertainment in hard times. Since he stole from banks, he was called a Robin Hood, though he wasn't known for giving to the poor.

He'd gone to a picture show at the Biograph Theatre not far from our neighborhood. With him were two bad women, and one of them tipped off the cops, who filled him full of lead on the sidewalk. Then, to prove they'd finally nailed John Dillinger, the police put his body on display in the morgue basement. People trooped past for a look. Women dipped their handkerchiefs in his bloody wounds for souvenirs. But he was so bloated and shot up that some people said it wasn't Dillinger at all. Rumor had it that he was holed up somewhere.

Mary Alice and I had sulked because neither Mother nor Dad would take us to view the riddled corpse. Recalling to ourselves Shotgun Cheatham, we thought we could take it. When we got back to school in September, everybody would say they'd seen the cadaver. It was a once-in-a-lifetime opportunity lost.

"I'd have took you," Grandma said. We didn't doubt it. Grandma wouldn't have minded a look for herself at all that remained of John Dillinger.

Mary Alice and I went upstairs to sort out our clothes from the single suitcase. She was getting particular about how everything she wore had to be hung up on a hanger just so. "Grandma's missing Mrs. Wilcox," she mentioned.

"Are you kidding?" I said. "She's Grandma's worst enemy. She says Mrs. Wilcox's tongue is attached in the middle and flaps at both ends. The town'll be quieter without her, and Grandma will like that."

"You don't know anything," Mary Alice said. "Men don't have any idea about women."

So I loped uptown by myself, heading for Veech's Gas and Oil, which was man's country. Ray Veech ran the garage when his dad was farming, and I thought I had some business with him.

The town was half-asleep with August and the depression. A checker game was going on in The Coffee Pot Cafe as I went past, but nothing else. A knot of people outside Moore's Store waited for the day-old bread to go half-price.

In the window of Stubbs & Askew, the insurance agency, you could put up handbills. The biggest was a drawing of the giant farm implement shed that Deere &

Company was proposing to put up on the block where the old brickyard had been.

Next to it a handbill advertised a rummage sale at the United Brethren Church:

BRING ❧ BUY
Treasures, Trash, Bric-a-Brac
Down-to-Earth Prices
Lunch Provided by Our Ladies' Circle

The last handbill was a schedule of the movies the Lions Club was showing at their outdoor picture show. They weren't new movies. Some of them weren't even talkies. It looked like a slow week.

I crossed the Wabash tracks past the grain elevator on my way to Veech's garage, eating the dust of the trucks hauling in the beans. Veech's garage had been the blacksmith shop, and they still kept the anvil inside. Now it was a one-pump filling station with an outdoor lift. I blundered along toward it. Then the dust cleared, and I saw her.

It was love at first sight, like I'd been waiting for her all my life. She stood on the pavement in front of Veech's, shimmering in her loveliness. And so graceful she might glide past me as if I wasn't there, leaving me in the dust.

She was a showroom-fresh Terraplane 8 from the Hudson Motor Car Company. A four-door sedan, tan, with red stripping and another touch of red at the hubcaps. Tears sprang and my eyes stung. I couldn't help it. My hands curled like I had her steering wheel in my grip.

No car company had an agency in Grandma's town, not

even Ford. But Veech's would order you a car. Ray'd said nobody had bought one in two years. He ducked out from under an ancient Locomobile up on the lift, working a greasy rag over his big hands.

Ray was seventeen and man-sized, and I'd worked hard to know him because I wanted him to teach me how to drive. He'd given me a couple of lessons last summer, but he wanted two dollars for the full course.

People around here didn't overreact even when they hadn't seen you for a year. Ray jerked a thumb back at the Locomobile he'd been working under. "Threw a rod."

I nodded like I knew.

But I couldn't take my eyes off the Terraplane. "Somebody order it?"

Ray rubbed his stubbled chin with the back of his hand in a way I admired. "Who's got seven hundred and ninety-five dollars? This baby's top-of-the-line. Son, it's got a radio."

I wanted to ask him if he'd driven it. But that was too close to asking him for a ride and a lesson. We both knew I didn't have two dollars.

"Hudson's sending out their new Terraplane models to drum up interest. It's the make Dillinger drove to outrun the cops. But, hey, you'd know that," Ray said. "You probably took a gander at the body the Chicago cops put on display. You reckon it was really Dillinger?"

I shrugged. I could see this was the summer when I missed out on everything.

That night after supper Grandma said, "I suppose you kids want to go to the picture show," meaning she wanted to go to the picture show. We were willing, though going to the pictures for us was the Oriental Theater in Chicago, featuring a first-run movie, a pipe organ, and a stage show with a dog act.

It was different at Grandma's. On Wednesday nights the Lions Club sponsored the picture show in the park. They put up canvas walls, so it was like a tent without a roof. You sat on benches, and they showed the movie on a sheet hung from the branch of a tree. Everybody but Baptists came. Admission was a nickel a head or a can of food for the hungry. Grandma took a quart Mason jar of her beets, and we three got in on that.

Since nobody liked sitting behind Grandma, we settled on the back row. There was some socializing she didn't take part in. Then the projectionist got the film threaded, and the show started. Mary Alice had been hoping for a Shirley Temple, but it was a Dracula, not too old, starring Bela Lugosi.

I have to say, it got to me. All those living dead people with black lips. When Dracula turned into a bat at the window, the night behind him merged with the night around us. It was a good audience for a horror picture. Several people screamed, and once a whole bench turned over. A night breeze sighed in the tree, making the screen waver. Mary Alice kept her eyes shut through most of it. Grandma barely blinked.

Afterward, we walked home in the dark. Mary Alice stuck close to Grandma, and I wasn't far off myself. The town was just one shadow after another. When a big lilac bush threw leaf patterns on the walk ahead of us, Grandma shied like a horse. Then we came to an old oak tree growing close to the road. Grandma pulled back and edged around it like Count Dracula was standing on the other side, in a cape.

Two or three years earlier we'd have thought the movie had spooked Grandma. Now we wondered if she was trying to spook us.

When we were safely inside at home, she made a business of latching the screen door. Then she looked meaningfully at the window over by the sink, like Dracula's electric eyes might be staring in, out of his terrible fanged face. Mary Alice and I were frozen to the linoleum in spite of ourselves.

"Grandma, there aren't such things as vampires, are there?" Mary Alice asked. Did she want to know, or was she testing Grandma? Every summer Mary Alice seemed to pick up another of Grandma's traits.

"Vampires? No. The only bloodsuckers is the banks." Grandma stroked her chins. "Movies is all pretend. They're made in California, you know. But they prove a point. Make something *seem* real, and people will believe it. The public will swallow anything."

That seemed her last word for the night. Now Mary Alice and I had to stumble up that long staircase to the darkness above. Being the man of the family, I ought to have gone first, but didn't.

"Sweet dreams," Grandma said behind us.

It was a long night, and hot. Mary Alice shut her window to keep vampire bats out. I know because I heard her closing hers when I was closing mine.

The next morning, after that restless night, I said to Grandma at the breakfast table, "I need two bucks bad."

"Who don't?" Grandma said. "What for?"

"Driving lessons, and Ray Veech wants two dollars to teach me."

"What do you want to learn to drive for anyway?" she said. "Don't you go around Chicago in taxicabs and trolleys?"

I couldn't explain it to Grandma. I was getting too old to be a boy, and driving meant you were a man. Something like that. I shrugged, and she slid a belly-busting breakfast in front of me.

Mary Alice turned up, looking like the ghost of herself. She was pale-faced with bags under her eyes. Though glad to see daylight, she was worn to a frazzle.

"Anyhow," Grandma said, "you don't have time for driving lessons. I want you two to poke around in the attic. I can't get up there anymore. You have to climb up through a trapdoor in the closet."

"What are we looking for?"

"Oh, I don't know. Any old rummage for the church sale."

So Grandma, who didn't take part in community activities, wanted to go to the rummage sale. She ate with the fork in one hand, the knife in the other. Then she looked up like she was having one of her sudden thoughts.

"Tell you what. Find that old stovepipe hat up there. It belonged to a preacher who knew my maw and paw. He was visiting one time, trying to convert them, and he dropped dead on the parlor rug. They kept his stovepipe hat on their hat rack ever after, to remember him by. I stuck it up there. Get it down. I saw a picture in the paper of John D. Rockefeller in a hat like that. They may be coming back in style."

I doubted that last part. But Mary Alice and I dragged a ladder upstairs. Grandma followed as far as the second floor to show us where the trapdoor was. We were disappearing up into the attic when below us she said, "Watch yourselves. I might have bats in my belfry."

We weren't familiar with attics, but this one wasn't too crowded. Grandma used up more than she saved. There were some three-legged chairs and a dress dummy half her size and some coal-oil lamps from olden times. Mary Alice dodged cobwebs and tried not to brush against anything. "I hate it up here," she said. But then we started going through a couple of old steamer trunks.

I pulled a big furry buffalo robe out of mine. "What about this?"

Mary Alice shrank. "Don't touch it. It's awful. It's got living things in it."

She was right. Things with wings. I put it aside. Then I came to some baby clothes, maybe Dad's, nothing too likely even for a rummage sale.

Mary Alice's trunk was full of paper: yellowed *Farm Journal*s and buttons on cardboard and a ton of dress patterns. Then she gasped.

In her hand was an ancient valentine, a big heart surrounded by paper lace. The motto on it read:

**WHEN CUPID SENDS HIS ARROW HOME,
I HOPE IT MRS. YOU.**

It was signed with a question mark.

"But, Joey, who was it sent *to?*" Mary Alice wondered.

"Grandma, I guess."

"She got *valentines?*" Mary Alice and I stared at each other.

Then she found another one, also ancient, but without the lace:

**WHEN YOU'RE OLD AND THINK YOU'RE SWEET,
TAKE OFF YOUR SHOES AND SMELL YOUR FEET.**

"That sounds more like it," Mary Alice said.

A voice of doom echoed up from the trapdoor. "You find that stovepipe hat yet?"

I jumped and so did Mary Alice. The lid on her trunk dropped down on her head.

Grandma was standing right under the trapdoor, listening to us and waiting for the stovepipe hat.

"I really, really hate this attic," Mary Alice said, whispering.

The hat was in my trunk. I handed it down to Grandma.

"It's getting too hot up here," Mary Alice said. "And all these dress patterns are from before the war." But out of the bottom of her trunk she pulled up an old quilt. It was so worn, you could see through it. Its pattern was fancy, but faded.

"How about this?" she said to me. She was looking around the hem to see if the quilt maker had stitched in her initials, but the edges were all fraying away.

"What is it?" said the trapdoor.

"An old quilt," we both yelled down.

"I forgot about that," Grandma hollered back. "My aunt Josie Smull pieced that quilt. Drop it down."

I did, and Grandma said, "Keep at it." We listened to her trudge away.

Other trunks were tucked away under the eaves, so it took us all morning to go through everything. But we didn't find anything else any sane person would want in a thousand years.

That afternoon we walked uptown and a block beyond to the United Brethren Church. We weren't going for the lunch the Ladies' Circle was selling. We ate at home, but Grandma said they'd be offering free lemonade. She'd taken off her apron and wore a hat. Not her fine, fair-going hat. This was the one she gardened and fished in, nibbled at the brim. She'd stuck a fresh peony at the front of the crown to dress it up. She strolled along over the occasional sidewalks with the preacher's stovepipe hat in a grocery bag. Mary Alice wore her straw hat and a dress because we were going to church, more or less. I brought up the rear with Aunt Josie Smull's quilt folded over my sweating arm.

"What's a church rummage sale like anyway?" Mary Alice asked.

"Ever been in a henhouse?" Grandma said.

The sale was in the church basement. The air was battered by funeral parlor fans, and ladies were picking over long tables. Some were still bringing in their treasures and trash. Others were snatching things up and taking them to the cashier's card table to pay for them. A sharp scent of potato salad hung in the air, but the Ladies' Circle had cleared away lunch. Now they were bringing out pitchers of free lemonade.

Everybody looked up when Grandma loomed into the room, as people always did. Several pulled back, but a tall, strict-looking lady came forth. "Why, goodness, it's Mrs. Dowdel," she said.

Grandma made short work of her by handing over the grocery bag and nodding at the quilt, which I offered up.

Mary Alice went for a look at the merchandise. But the tables were surrounded by flying elbows, so I settled next to Grandma. She was on a folding chair, pouring herself a glass of lemonade. She had a way of sitting with her feet apart and her hands on her knees. After a good long swig of lemonade, she observed the scene. In fact, she was biding her time. Somehow I knew this.

A flurry began at the other end of a table. From their hats, they were all town ladies, not country. A hiss of whispers whipped up into raised voices. Grandma sat on, at her ease.

Then the strict lady in charge, who was Mrs. Earl T. Askew, came through the crowds, heading for us. Mrs. Askew's face had gone vampire white.

Bending to Grandma, she spoke in low, urgent tones. "Mrs. Dowdel, I feel I must tell you that Mrs. L. J. Weidenbach, the banker's wife, has offered *fifteen dollars* for that stovepipe hat."

She stared at Grandma for a reaction and got nothing back.

"Mrs. Dowdel, are you one-hundred-percent sure you want to part with that hat?"

"It don't belong to me." Grandma made a small gesture. "I have an idea it was in with some other old stuff Effie Wilcox threw away when the bank run her out of town."

Mrs. Askew's gaze was electric. "Other old stuff?" She seemed to have trouble breathing.

Grandma nodded. "Just old clutter Effie had found in the house back when she moved in."

Mrs. Askew pivoted like a dancer and was gone. Already Mrs. L. J. Weidenbach was over at the cashier, peeling off five-dollar bills as fast as she could dig them out of her pocketbook.

Oh, Grandma, I thought, what have you done?

Mrs. Askew plunged back. Aunt Josie Smull's quilt was clutched in her arms like a long-lost child. "Mrs. Dowdel," she said, "oh, Mrs. Dowdel, are you one-hundred-percent—"

Grandma took the quilt onto her lap, smoothed it out, and looked it over. A crowd gathered. There in the corner, worked in faded thread, initials had magically appeared on the fraying hem:

M.T.L.

Suddenly, Mrs. Weidenbach appeared, gripping the preacher's stovepipe hat. She went right for Mrs. Askew. "What have you got there? Let me—"

"Not so fast, Wilhelmina," Mrs. Askew snapped. "I

seen—saw it first." She swept up the quilt that Grandma gladly surrendered.

"What are those initials?" Mrs. Weidenbach was beside herself. "Oh my stars and garters! M.T. L. Mary Todd Lincoln! And I've got Abe Lincoln's own stovepipe hat. His name's lettered in on the sweatband!"

Two things happened that next morning. A car from out of town backfired in the vicinity of the bank, and everybody on the sidewalk dropped down and grabbed gravel. Who knew but what John Dillinger was alive and well and up to his old tricks?

The other thing was a knock at Grandma's front door right after breakfast. Mary Alice and I followed when she went to answer it, opening to a stringy young guy in a seersucker suit.

"Well, Otis," she said, "what?"

"Ma'am," he said, "Mr. Weidenbach would be pleased if you could spare him a moment of your time at your earliest convenience."

Grandma stepped back and clutched her throat, showing shock. "Don't tell me the bank's failed. Banks is failing all over. Had I better draw out my funds? Is there time?"

"No, ma'am, the bank's still in business." Otis looked down at his boots. "Your seventeen dollars is safe."

"You give me a turn!" she said, slapping at her bosom and shutting the door in his face.

She waited an hour and a half. Then she put on her gardening hat and went uptown to the bank. Mary Alice and

I went with her. When we got to the business block, people were still just getting up off the sidewalk. The bank was store-sized, and the only teller was Otis, back in his cage. He waved us through to the rear office, beside the safe.

I'd never seen Mr. Weidenbach before, but this couldn't have been one of his better days. Over his head on the wall above the desk was a widemouthed bass, stuffed. "You will have to excuse me," he boomed, showing us chairs. "This crackbrained rumor that Dillinger is still alive is doing our business no good."

"If it's a rumor at all," said Grandma, on her dignity and then some. "A rumor is sometimes truth on the trail."

"I am interested to hear you say so, Mrs. Dowdel." The banker pulled the purse strings of his mouth taut. "It brings us to the point."

"Get right to it," Grandma said.

"Certain items supposedly from the estate of President and Mrs. Abraham Lincoln have surfaced in a house the bank is forced to foreclose on. Do you grasp what this could mean, Mrs. Dowdel?"

Grandma thought she did. "I expect the state will take that land and restore the house as a museum. I hear a rumor Lincoln debated Douglas in that very parlor. Rumor has it he split the rails for the fence that used to enclose the brickyard."

"And who's been circulating such cockeyed rumors?" The banker turned a deeper color.

"Who knows where a rumor starts?" Grandma mused. "Who knows where it'll end? They've very likely heard it at the statehouse in Springfield by now. I have an idea they'll send over a historian any day now to snoop."

"Mrs. Dowdel, the bank has signed papers with Deere and Company to build an implement shed across that entire property and the site of the old brickyard too. Any delay throws a monkey wrench in the deal. Better times are on the way, and what's good for a bank is good for the community."

"But a nice state park wouldn't be bad either," Grandma pondered. "We could all set out on summer evenings, recalling Honest Abe. That park we got now is just wasteland the Wabash Railroad didn't want."

Mr. Weidenbach's gaping mouth hung near his blotter now. He had his desktop in a death grip. "Mrs. Dowdel, you falsified those so-called Lincoln items. They're bogus. I could have the law on you."

"That's right." Grandma gazed above him at the wide-mouthed bass. "The banker throws the poor old widder in the pokey. That'll look real good for your business."

Mr. Weidenbach was smaller now, deflated. "Mrs. Dowdel," he said in a voice strangled with emotion, "help me out of this. I'm in too deep with John Deere. I got to go forward because I can't do otherwise."

"Lop off your back end," Grandma said.

"I beg your pardon?"

"Build a shorter implement shed over the old brickyard, and leave Effie Wilcox's house be."

A glimmer of hope showed in the banker's hard eye.

"I suppose we could go back to the drawing board and reallocate our square footage."

"Do that," Grandma said. "And one more thing. You

give Effie Wilcox back her house, free and clear. It isn't worth nothing anyway—apart from its historical value."

"Mrs. Dowdel, that's not business," the banker said. "That's blackmail."

"What's the difference?" Grandma said.

A silence was observed. Then banker Weidenbach turned up his hands. "All right. It's Mrs. Wilcox's house, free and clear. But you'll have to confess you falsified those so-called Lincoln items. Fair's fair."

"Oh well." Grandma sketched a casual pattern in the air with one hand. "We can get that rumor going right now. Effie didn't mean to put Lincoln's name in the stovepipe hat. I—she just lettered in 'A Lincoln' to mean it was the kind of hat he wore."

Mary Alice and I exchanged a look across Grandma.

"And that M.T. L. on the quilt. Pshaw!" Grandma said. "Effie Wilcox had a cousin, name of Maude Teeter Lingenbloom. That's M.T. L. for you."

Mr. Weidenbach replied in an exhausted voice, "I'll get the word out."

Grandma was on her feet now. She patted the bun of her back hair under the nibbled brim. "Free and clear, you got that?" she said to Mr. Weidenbach. "Effie don't make no more payments on that house." Then as if a sudden thought struck her, she nudged me. "And you can give this boy here a two-dollar bill." She nudged Mary Alice. "And fair's fair. Give this girl two dollars too."

"That's big money for young'uns," the banker said. "Shall I draw it out of your account, Mrs. Dowdel?"

"No, you double-dealing, four-flushing old cootie," she replied. "You can draw it out of your own wallet. Any man with a wife who'll pay fifteen dollars for an old preacher's moth-eaten stovepipe hat has four bucks to spare."

Silent wars seemed to wage in Mr. Weidenbach's brain. Then he pulled his wallet out of his hip pocket. He kept a bootlace tied around it. We watched as he drew out a pair of two-dollar bills and handed them to Mary Alice and me. And heaven help us, we took them.

Rumors are things with wings too. The rumor that I had two dollars reached Ray Veech before I could. He was going to have to give me my driving lessons at the end of the day when he was sure his dad was out on the farm, milking. Otherwise, his dad would take a cut. Also, we needed to use the Terraplane 8, which was strictly forbidden under an agreement with the Hudson Motor Car Company.

I started off to Ray's that evening with a two-dollar bill in my jeans and a song in my heart. I felt like I was six feet tall and shaved. My right hand played through the gearshift positions, and I was ready.

Then Grandma called out after me that she and Mary Alice were going along for the ride.

And how could I explain to Grandma that learning to drive was kind of a sacred thing, and you don't want your kid sister and your grandma along?

Grandma filled most of the backseat of the Terraplane. Mary Alice sat beside her with an unspent two-dollar bill in her pocketbook. From Grandma, Mary Alice was learning thrift. She could squeeze two cents till they begged for mercy, let alone two dollars.

Ray was up front with me, and I was behind the wheel. I'd crept out of town in second gear, and now Ray was showing me third. I knew if I got so much as a scratch on the fender, I was a dead man, so that kept me alert. And I stayed to the crown of the road, hoping not to meet anything oncoming. Visors flipped down to keep the setting sun out of our eyes. It was a car with every refinement. And though I wasn't steering straight yet, I was beginning to get the feel of the thing. The Terraplane and I were becoming as one. I no longer let the motor die at crossroads.

After we made it across the plank bridge over Salt Creek, Ray reached down and turned the radio to WGN. Out of static came the sweet strains of cocktail hour music from the Empire Room of the Palmer House Hotel in Chicago, Illinois. It was a modern miracle. Here we were skimming along a country road out past Cowgills' Dairy Farm, and we were hearing music being played in the Chicago Loop.

Grandma's head appeared between Ray's and mine. "What in the Sam Hill is that noise?" she said.

Ray indicated the radio.

"Shut it off," she said. "Let's listen to the country."

So we did. Since a Terraplane is another thing with wings, I edged up to twenty-five miles an hour, watching the needle rise. Over the purr of the motor we heard a wind pump squeaking as it turned and a calf bawling and the katydids starting up in a grove of walnut trees. I see us yet, chasing the setting sun down the ribbon of road between the bean rows, in the Terraplane. I thought it was about as fine a car as they'd ever make. I'm not so sure it wasn't.

Grandma came to the depot with us on the day we were going home. But she wasn't there to see us off. She was there to meet Mrs. Effie Wilcox, who was coming home to her house.

The Wabash Blue Bird didn't exactly stop at Grandma's town. It only hesitated. As we were struggling to climb on, Mrs. Wilcox was struggling to get off. Her valise was full to bursting, and her eyes were everywhere, so I don't know if she spotted Grandma at first.

But then somehow Mary Alice and I and our suitcase were on board, and Mrs. Wilcox was on the platform, and the Blue Bird was pulling out. Grandma didn't wave. Mrs. Wilcox was telling her something. But we waved anyway.

Centennial Summer

———⟨∾∾∾⟩———

1935

I was fifteen the last summer we went down to Grandma's. Mary Alice was thirteen, so we both thought we were too old for this sort of thing. Next year I'd be in line for a summer job in Chicago, if I could find one. Mary Alice was about to sail into eighth grade, which put her in shooting distance of high school.

We both assumed an air of weary worldliness as we climbed down off the Wabash Blue Bird one last time. But the train hadn't pulled out before we noticed a difference.

The depot was swagged in red, white, and blue bunting. Where the old DRIFTERS KEEP MOVING sign used to hang, a new billboard in fancy lettering read:

"You're in trouble right there," Mary Alice remarked to me.

We both sighed. We were still kids, so we liked everything to stay the same. Now the whole town seemed to be up to something.

"What's it all about?" we asked Grandma when we got to her house.

"The Centennial Celebration? Nothin' but an excuse for people to mill around, waste time, and make horses' patooties of themselves. I hope I never see another one."

Considering that the next centennial celebration would be in the year 2035, we didn't think Grandma would have a problem with it.

Over dinner she added, "There'll be a parade, of course. We can watch it from the porch."

As we tucked into big slabs of sour cream raisin pie, Grandma observed, "They're putting on a talent show. We might look in on that. We won't have to stay till the end."

Then after dinner she said, "You two are going to have to climb up to the attic and go through them trunks again."

"What for?" said Mary Alice, who hated the attic.

"Well for pity sakes," Grandma said, quite impatient, "you and me's going to have to wear old-time long dresses." She aimed a fork at me. "And you're going to have to wear a historical getup too."

At least she didn't comment on the fact that I couldn't raise a beard, though her glance skimmed my chin.

"Grandma." Mary Alice clutched her head. "What's happening?"

"It's the Centennial Celebration," Grandma said. "We're all going back to the old days and the old ways for a week."

"Grandma," I said, "you never gave up any of the old ways."

"Ha," she said. "A lot you know. And while you're up in the attic, look around for that old churn. It's how we used to make butter. Bring it down."

The attic was hot as hinges, and nothing had changed since last year. "For pity sakes, don't mention those old coal-oil lamps," Mary Alice whispered to me. "She'll shut off the electricity and make us use them."

We made a quick survey of the trunk full of dress patterns and the one with the buffalo robe in it. In old suit boxes under the eaves we found folded clothes that went back before the war, way back. Mary Alice's forehead was greasy now, and we were both down on all fours, pawing through strange old dresses and funny shoes.

"What are you finding?" came Grandma's voice from below.

"Grandma, you're not going to be able to get into any

of these old clothes," Mary Alice hollered down.

"No, but you can," Grandma hollered back.

I grinned. Mary Alice wilted.

Then she came on another box with a lot of brittle old tissue paper inside. "Aha!" she said, drawing out an old black coat with braid around the lapels. Then a waistcoat with many buttons. Then a shirt with a high collar attached by another button. A pair of drainpipe pants. A string tie, a derby hat.

"Made for you!" Mary Alice crowed. She was beginning to enjoy herself, I was sorry to see.

"I'll look like Broshear the undertaker in that stuff," I said. "I'll look like a horse's patootie. I want to go home."

Mary Alice burrowed under more tissue in the box.

"Oh, look." She held up a dress finer than the others, white going yellow with age. It had a high collar of flaking lace.

"Made for you," I said, but Mary Alice didn't mind. She ran a careful hand over it. "Seed pearls," she murmured.

In another box there was nothing but old cut-velvet curtains with fringe at the bottom. "Just curtains," I said.

"Cut-velvet with fringe?" Grandma thundered from below.

"Yes," we yelled back.

"Bring 'em down," she roared. "And don't forget the churn."

After Mary Alice twice said she was so hot she thought she might throw up, we left. We took everything we'd found with us: clothes, curtains, churn—half the attic. Grandma was nowhere about.

"Let's see if these clothes fit," Mary Alice said.

"Let's not."

"Joey, you know we're going to have to wear this stuff," she said.

I went to my room and skinned off my shirt and pants. Then I put on the old white shirt with the stiff front. It came to my knees, but I could push the sleeves up. The drainpipe pants were a fit when I gave the legs extra cuff. It took me awhile, buttoning up the vest, and I liked the coat. It gave me shoulders. The string tie was like a boot-lace, so I could tie it by looking in the mirror. Then I thought, why not? I put on the derby hat. It went down to my ears and balanced there.

I strolled out into the hall, and stepped back. Mary Alice stood there, posing in the old white dress. She was beginning to develop a figure, more or less. But the dress had a figure of its own. Narrow in the waist, generous above.

"I stuck in some tissue paper," she said quietly, glancing down. Her chin balanced on the high lace collar, and she reached down into the folds of the skirt that swirled to the floor. "But there's something wrong," she said. "Behind."

"Turn around," I said. The dress fitted her like a glove, above the waist.

"What's all this?" She patted an enormous artificial behind, swagged with seed pearls.

"I think they called it a bustle," I said.

"But how did she sit down?"

"Search me," I said.

Mary Alice turned back. "You look good," she said. "The hat's dumb, but you look good."

"So do you." Though I'd never noticed before, Mary Alice was going to be quite a nice-looking girl. I supposed boys would be hanging around her pretty soon. It was a thought I'd never had.

"Let's go show Grandma," she said.

With a dainty gesture, she lifted her skirts as she started down the stairs. I followed, sweaty in two wool layers. Grandma wasn't in the kitchen or the front room. We found her in the little sewing room off her downstairs bedroom. She was bending over her old treadle Singer sewing machine, threading a bobbin.

Mary Alice rustled her bustle in, and I followed. Just before Grandma turned to see us, I took off the derby hat. I put it in the crook of my arm, like we were an old tintype picture in a fancy frame. Mary Alice held out the silky skirt. Grandma turned around from the sewing machine, and froze.

An instant of silence fell when you could hear a wasp on the windowsill. Then Grandma swept the spectacles off her nose. She wiped a hand quickly over her eyes. We quaked. We hadn't seen her like this before.

"You give me a turn," she said. She put her hand out to us and took it back. "I thought it was me and Dowdel on our wedding day."

Of course—these were their wedding clothes. They'd lived together all these years, separate in their box together.

"How did you sit?" Mary Alice said, turning to show the bustle.

"To one side," Grandma said, "on one of your haunches. Then you let the skirts fan out on the floor. I only wore it that one day." She couldn't take her eyes off us, and her eyes were full.

We three were at the breakfast table the next morning, in our regular clothes, when a sharp footstep sounded on the back porch.

A rounded figure with a head cocked like a bird filled the screen door. It was Mrs. L. J. Weidenbach, the banker's wife.

Grandma looked up from her breakfast, scrapple and corn syrup with sides of bacon. "Only ten after six," Grandma muttered, "and she's already girdled and gallivantin'."

Mrs. Weidenbach must have been desperate, because she'd lowered herself to come to Grandma's back door. "Oh, Mrs. Dowdel," she said through screen wire, "you see before you a woman at the end of her rope."

"I wish," Grandma mumbled.

Mrs. Weidenbach dared to open the screen door and slip inside on her teetery high-heeled shoes. Dad had taught me to stand up when a lady enters the room, but a look from Grandma kept me in my place.

"Mrs. Dowdel, as head of the Ladies' Hospitality Committee for the Centennial Celebration, I have come to fling myself at your feet. We of the committee have worked our fingers to the bone to make the celebration worthy of the town's traditions. Now on the eve of the event, my committee members are dropping like flies. You will have heard how Mrs. Askew has been brought low." Mrs. Weidenbach's voice fell. "Female troubles."

Grandma's specs were riding down her nose. She looked up over them. "Oh yes. Cora Askew's insides has been given a public airing."

"And then there is Mrs. Forrest Pugh's nervous condition," Mrs. Weidenbach sighed. "Mrs. Dowdel, I'll put it to you straight. Our committee has more than it can manage—handing out programs, setting up chairs, arranging for prizes, keeping the ladies' public rest room tidy. It is not glorious work, Mrs. Dowdel, but it is meaningful. I thought you might step in and lend us a hand. We understand that at your time of life, you are not as active as you once were. But we are in great hopes you will rise to the occasion."

I thought Grandma might rise to the occasion and throw the kitchen table at Mrs. Weidenbach. Mary Alice and I got ready to run.

Mrs. Weidenbach's hand plunged into her bosom and drew up a lacy hanky. "I can do no more," she said, dabbing at her mouth. "I will have my hands full with Daddy during the celebration itself. As a ninety-year-old veteran of the Civil War, Daddy is bound to carry off the honor of being Oldest Settler, and he will need all my support. But he's bound to win." Mrs. Weidenbach looked suddenly uncertain. "Unless Aunt Puss Chapman—"

"Naw." Grandma waved a strip of bacon. "You couldn't blast Aunt Puss off her place with a charge of dynamite."

"Well, then," Mrs. Weidenbach said, reassured. "And I will have to be on hand for the talent show," she continued. "My nephew is entering it with a dramatic reading, and I must be there for the boy."

"Ah," Grandma said. "Let me see if I heard right. At my time of life, my hearing isn't what it was."

Mary Alice and I stared at each other. Of all her whoppers, this was Grandma's crowning achievement. She had ears on her like an Indian scout.

"You want me to swab out toilets while you run your old daddy for Oldest Settler and your nephew for public speaker. Or did my ears deceive me?"

"Well, I wouldn't have put it quite like that." Mrs. Weidenbach dabbed all around her neck.

"I'm busy as a bird dog myself these days," Grandma said. "I've got my grandkids visiting, as you may have noticed. And my tomatoes are coming on. I'm rushed off my feet." Grandma sprawled in her chair, the picture of ease.

"You don't mean you're canning tomatoes on Centennial week!" Mrs. Weidenbach goggled.

"Tomatoes wait for no man," Grandma said, gazing at the door.

Defeated, Mrs. Weidenbach took the hint and retreated. We listened to her heels pecking off the porch. I wiped the last scrap of scrapple around my plate in the corn syrup. Mary Alice examined her fingernails, waiting. Grandma was deep in thought, and we were passing the time until she came to a conclusion.

She slapped the oilcloth at last. "No rest for the weary," she said, climbing to her feet. She ran a hand down the small of her back, though it was none too small. "Not enough hours in the day."

"We picking tomatoes, Grandma?" I asked, testing her.

"What?" she said.

She glanced down at Mary Alice. "Bring your tap shoes?"

"My *tap* shoes!" Mary Alice clutched her head, which she often did these days. "Grandma, I haven't taken tap since I was a *kid*."

"Give it up, did you?" Grandma said.

"*Ages* ago." Mary Alice sniffed. "I'm taking ballroom dancing now, to get ready for high-school mixers and formal and semiformal evenings."

Grandma pondered, fingering her chins.

Then she said to me, "Find my gum boots. We're goin' to high grass and tall timber. Take us the better part of the day to get there and back on shank's ponies." Which meant we'd be walking.

When I didn't find her gum boots in the cellar, she sent me to the cobhouse. As I passed through the kitchen, I noticed Grandma and Mary Alice had their heads together, conspiring.

The only light in the cobhouse came from the open door. But I could see the Phantom Brakeman's old overcoat hanging on a peg. Under it stood Grandma's gum boots. When I reached down for them, a boot moved.

Remembering cottonmouths, I recoiled. My hands were in my armpits when I heard a sound. One of the boots mewed. I'd forgotten about the old tomcat. But then he'd have jumped at me by now, if he'd been around. A kitten's face appeared out of the top of the boot. Pointy ears, whiskers, big green eyes. She mewed at me again and tried to get a paw up. I reached down for her. She was gray with a white bib and boots. She only weighed ounces, and she kept her claws in when I tucked her in my arm and carried her back to the house with the gum boots.

In the kitchen Grandma had her gardening hat on, with the chigger veil. She was packing our lunch, with a couple of early tomatoes and some salt for them in a twist of paper. I drew nigh and planted the kitten on the table beside her.

"Get that thing out of the house!" she barked. But neither the kitten nor I was fooled. The kitten butted Grandma's hand. Then she rubbed herself along Grandma's arm, and Grandma let her.

"Got a new pet?" I inquired.

"Chicago people have pets," she said. "But there's a new litter living down in the cobhouse now, and I let 'em. They keep down the vermin. Don't need all of them though." Gently, she lifted the kitten and put her in the hamper with our lunch. "We'll drown this one in the crick on our way," she said. But I wasn't worried.

"What happened to the old cat?" I asked, meaning the jumping tom.

"Got in front of the Cannonball," Grandma said briefly.

She was sitting to tug her gum boots on now, and she was already wearing men's pants under apron and dress.

"Grandma, are we going out to see Aunt Puss Chapman?" I said, trying to see a little bit ahead.

"We're going farther out in the sticks than that," she said, grunting.

"What for?"

"To see if an old feller name of Uncle Grady Griswold's

still living. And his wife, Aunt Mae."

By now I knew that not everybody around here called "Uncle" or "Aunt" was necessarily *your* uncle or aunt. "Why do we want to know?"

"Because if he's alive, Uncle Grady'd be a hundred and three years old."

The sun had already begun to punish us by the time we'd crossed the bridge over Salt Creek. I was carrying the hamper, and mews came from within. Grandma had forgotten to drown the kitten. We walked a long way over roads we'd skimmed in the Terraplane 8. Mary Alice wasn't with us. She was elsewhere. Mary Alice was up to something.

By noon we were nearly out of the county. We'd crossed Route 36. But Grandma trudged on. We ate our lunch in a pasture. The kitten climbed out and fed from our hands. Then she stalked around in the weeds, teaching herself to jump at butterflies. When it was time to go, she climbed back into the hamper. We cut across the fields from there, to a little house at the end of a faint lane.

Somebody still lived there. Chickens were in the brooder house, and the garden was in and weeded. Hollyhocks stood guard along the fence. Grandma pushed open the front door.

It was a parlor from some other time, with faded love knots in the wallpaper. Beside a cold stove sat an old lady. On the other side in a rocker sat the oldest man on earth, in a stocking cap.

Grandma sighed with satisfaction to see them both breathing. Aunt Mae Griswold grinned at Grandma. Both her teeth gleamed in the gloom of the room.

"How you been, Aunt Mae?"

"Oh yes," Aunt Mae agreed. "Very warm for the time of year." She wore gardening gloves and a variety of shawls.

"How are your feet?" Grandma thundered at her. "Are they still swelling on you?"

"Not bad," Aunt Mae said. "They're still pretty good layers. We get eight or ten dozen eggs off them every day and sell what we don't eat to the Cowgills."

Grandma turned to Uncle Grady.

"Speak right up to him," Aunt Mae called out. "He's a little hard of hearing."

Uncle Grady Griswold was almost as small as he was old. The pom-pom on his stocking cap hung far down his humped shoulder. He was so old he'd have made Aunt Puss Chapman look like a young girl at her first party. He gazed uninterested up at Grandma.

"How you been, Uncle Grady?" she said, speaking up.

"Fair to piddling," he said weakly.

Grandma lifted the kitten out of the hamper by the scruff of its neck. "I brought you a mouser."

Uncle Grady blinked at the hanging kitten and seemed to rally. "Put her right here," he said, and Grandma lowered the kitten into his bony lap, where she offered her head for petting.

"Do you get up and around, Uncle Grady?"

"Oh yes," he said in a stronger voice. "I wrung the neck

off a chicken this morning before daylight."

"Did you have chicken for your dinner?"

"No." He shook his head. "She got away."

"Ah," Grandma said. "Listen, Uncle Grady. Do you still have your old army uniform?"

He started, and the kitten looked up in alarm. He waved two small, shriveled fists. "Has war been declared?" He'd have jumped out of his chair, ready to enlist, but Grandma put a hand on him.

"Nothin' like that," she said.

"Well, I'm ready," he piped up. "I'm cocked and primed. My full kit's in the bedroom there." He pointed a crooked finger. "We sleep downstairs now because Mae can't climb steps. She's getting on in years."

Grandma nodded me toward the bedroom. "Don't forget my sword!" Uncle Grady called after me, seeming not to wonder who I was. Aunt Mae looked on, interested.

I found his full kit: uniform, sword, boots and spurs, and a cap. They didn't smell very good, and they didn't look right to me.

"Grandma," I muttered, holding up the small coat. "There's something funny about this uniform." The only Civil War uniform I'd ever seen up close was on Mrs. L. J. Weidenbach's daddy. "Was Uncle Grady on our side?"

"Of course he was on our side," she said. "But he goes back before the Civil War. He was in the Mexican War."

"They winged me at the battle of Cerro Gordo," Uncle Grady offered.

I stared. We'd covered the Mexican War in school that year. "Grandma, the Mexican War started almost ninety years ago. Even if Uncle Grady is a hundred and three, he'd only have been about my age during that war."

"Well, maybe he was a little drummer boy," Grandma suggested.

"Rum-tum-tum," Uncle Grady said, playing an imaginary drum with invisible drumsticks.

Grandma turned to the other rocker. "Can I borrow Uncle Grady for the day on Saturday, Aunt Mae?" she howled.

"You sure can, honey," Aunt Mae said. "In fact, you can keep him!" She'd heard every word and grinned broadly.

On the first day of the Centennial Celebration the town began to fill up with merrymakers and the curious. People came in farm wagons and Fords from as far away as Bement and Tuscola. Grandma closed all her windows because the dust from the road never settled.

People came for the events, the tree-topping and chicken-plucking competitions, and the chili cook-off. They marveled at the flower show put on by the ladies of the United Brethren Church and the mother-daughter look-alike contest, the spelling bee, the Illinois Power and Light Company's display on rural electrification, and the three-legged race.

I hadn't seen hide nor hoof mark of Mary Alice all day. That evening Grandma and I had a quiet supper at the kitchen table, under the ceiling light and the fly-paper strips. This was the night of the talent show. I knew we were going, even after she poured a second cup of coffee and stifled a yawn like she was thinking of bed.

"Well, I guess you'll want to look in on the show," she remarked.

But I was fifteen now, and wise to her. I stifled a yawn. "Doesn't matter to me."

"We don't have to stay to the end." She was on her feet now, making short work of the dishes.

The stage was the bandstand in the park, lit with headlights running off car batteries. We chose a back bench because nobody wanted to sit behind Grandma. And we could see everybody from here. The audience was mostly town people because the farmers had all gone home to do their chores. But there was a good turnout. Mr. and Mrs. L. J. Weidenbach were up in the front row.

On a table by the bandstand waited the loving cup for first prize and the scrolls for second, third, and honorable mention. Just as the crowd was getting restless, the first act began, a man playing a musical saw. Grandma sat through that with both hands clamped on her knees. Afterward she remarked that it had been "more saw than music."

Then we had a barbershop quartet. Though they called themselves "The Sons of the Prairie Pioneers" and all wore beards, they were Mr. Earl T. Askew and three more of the sheriff's deputies. Practice had improved them some, and they didn't sing "The Night That Paddy Murphy Died" in mixed company. They did a medley that included "Just a Song at Twilight" and after a round of applause, came back for "Sweet Adeline."

Grandma wasn't about to clap for deputies. She began to fidget.

The vocal part of the program continued with the choir from Mrs. Effie Wilcox's church. They did "Sweet Hour of Prayer," "The Old Rugged Cross," and "I Come to the Garden Alone While the Dew Is Still on the Roses." These got no response from United Brethren members. But the choir returned for an encore anyway, with tambourines, to sing:

> *Swing low, sweet Chariot,*
> *And scoop me from the mire;*
> *Take me up to Glory,*
> *Snatched from Eternal Fire.*

If I hadn't known better, I'd have thought Grandma was ready to leave. She was fidgeting all over the bench. Then a boy clumped on the stage. He was about fifth grade or an overgrown fourth. His hair was parted in the middle, and he'd painted artificial freckles all over his moon face. His costume was high-topped shoes and old-time britches held up by one suspender. "That's my nephew, everybody!" Mrs. L. J. Weidenbach called out from the front row.

He cleared his throat and began to recite:

> *Ain't I glad I ain't a girl,*
> *Hands to wash and hair to curl,*
> *Skirts a-flappin' round my knees,*
> *Ain't I glad that that ain't me?*

The boy planted his fists on his pudgy hips and looked out over the audience.

> *Grandpa says it's just a chance*
> *That I got to wearin' pants,*
> *Says that when a kid is small,*
> *They puts dresses on 'em all.*

They that kicks and makes a noise
Gets promoted into boys.
Them that sits and twists their curls,
They just leaves them, calls them "girls."

He took his bow to a spatter of applause that grew. All of Mrs. Weidenbach's friends stood to clap, and they were joined by everybody who owed the bank money. The boy kept bowing.

"That made me about half-sick," Grandma remarked.

At this point we could have used an intermission. But Mrs. Merle Stubbs of the Ladies' Committee mounted the stage, carrying a portable Victrola. She threw wide its doors and wound it.

"Crank it up, Lula," somebody called out, and the crowd tittered. Mrs. Stubbs dropped a record on the turntable and withdrew. They'd have dimmed the lights now, but the car batteries were weakening anyway. Music from a full orchestra welled out of the Victrola. It was a waltz, "When I Grow Too Old to Dream, I'll Have You to Remember."

From nowhere a couple glided onto the bandstand stage. He was tall, dark, and handsome, and seemed to be wearing a tuxedo. In his big hands he held a girl. The vision of a girl. Headlights caught the glimmer of her white gown as he twirled her in easy circles. Her graceful hand held up her flowing skirts.

The crowd caught its breath. It was like a movie coming to life. The seed pearls on the girl's dress flashed pale fire. I looked again, and behind the careful makeup, below the swooped-up hair—it was Mary Alice. As she turned in the waltz, a bustle came into view.

I nudged Grandma hard. But she was completely caught up in the sight of Mary Alice sweeping around the stage in Grandma's own wedding gown.

But who was her partner? He was dipping her almost to the floor now, though you couldn't tell who was leading who. I squinted and saw it was Ray Veech.

Ray Veech, of Veech's Gas and Oil, and wearing Grandpa Dowdel's wedding suit with the cuffs let all the way down. Ray Veech, a man's man, who spent his life under cars with grease up to his elbows. Ray Veech and Mary Alice. My world tilted.

Now the waltz was winding down. Ray and Mary Alice came out even with it. Still clinging to one of his big hands, she collapsed to the floor in an elegant curtsey. Her skirts fanned out in every direction.

After a moment of stunned silence the crowd was on its feet. They were getting up on their benches and clapping over their heads in applause like summer thunder.

Grandma stood. Patting her back hair in a satisfied way, she said, "We don't need to stay to the end."

We were up way before daybreak on Saturday. While the dew was still on the roses, the road outside Grandma's house was thronged with people coming in from as far away now as Argenta and Farmer City for the parade. But we were working right up to the last minute on our float.

At the stroke of eleven the parade stepped off with the high-school bands of the three nearest towns with high schools. Next in the order of procession were five tractor-drawn hayframes jammed with members of the Piatt County Democratic Party. They were followed by Mr. L. J. Weidenbach in a decorated Hupmobile carrying all four Republicans.

The Odd Fellows' drum and bugle corps followed. On their heels, mounted, trotted the Anti-Horse-Thief Society members done up as old-time bounty hunters in big hats and drooping mustaches.

Then came the first float. Mrs. L. J. Weidenbach had outdone herself, aided by a club she belonged to, the Order of the Eastern Star. Their float was a flatbed International Harvester truck banked in flowers. In a kitchen chair sat Mrs. Weidenbach's old daddy in full Civil War blue and his decoration from the Grand Army of the Republic. He seemed to have no idea where he was. Surrounding him on the flatbed were Eastern Star ladies garbed in Grecian drapings. Mrs. L. J. Weidenbach was there too, in a vast hoopskirt, holding her daddy upright.

Above him a sign, roped in rambler roses, read:

OLDEST SETTLER IN THE COMMUNITY
❧ BORN 1845 ❧
DECORATED VETERAN OF THE CIVIL WAR

By rights, this float should have been followed by a marching platoon from the Woman's Christian Temperance Union carrying their sign:

STRONG DRINK IS A MOCKER

But somehow, our float cut in. It was another hayframe, this one from Cowgills' Dairy Farm. Flanking it on foot were the Cowgill brothers, who had all grown up to be good Christian men, except for Ernie, who was in jail. The horse that pulled our hayframe was the one that usually pulled the Cowgills' milk wagon. It had its work cut out for it because there was a lot happening on our float.

At the front was a sweating yellow mound that had been a cow carved out of butter before the sun got to it. Nearby stood Mary Alice in her ball gown, bowing to the crowd and holding up the loving cup for first prize in the talent show. I rode up there with her, wearing Grandpa Dowdel's wedding suit because Ray wouldn't ride on a float. Behind us sat Mrs. Effie Wilcox on a three-legged stool. She was demonstrating the use of a pioneer butter churn, and her eyes roamed all over the crowds beside the street.

At the back of the float was a throne, though it was only the platform rocker from Grandma's front room. On a pile of pillows to give him stature sat Uncle Grady Griswold in full uniform. The sun sparkled off the tip of the sword he held aloft. He could no more raise a beard than I could, so he looked like a beaming boy.

To lend him support, Grandma stood beside him, her feet planted wide. She was another Grandma, one we'd never seen before. Her costume was an enormous and complicated old-fashioned gown made out of cut-velvet and fringe. Its bustle overhung the rear of the hayframe, and the front of it scooped breathtakingly low on her bosom. She'd topped herself with Idella Eubanks's sunbonnet. Loose in her hand hung Grandpa Dowdel's twelve-gauge Winchester. After all, it was an antique.

Above them hung a sign, a sheet stretched between clothesline poles. It had taken me half the night to letter it:

UNCLE GRADY GRISWOLD
BORN 1832
AND WINGED IN THE MEXICAN WAR
BY FAR THE OLDEST SETTLER IN THE COMMUNITY

Just the sight of Grandma herself silenced the crowds. But by the time we were trundling past The Coffee Pot Cafe and Uncle Grady was brandishing his sword, the applause began.

Into Mary Alice's ear I muttered, "But why Ray Veech?"

"I saw possibilities in him," she said coolly, showing off her loving cup to the crowds.

"I didn't know he could dance."

"Dance?" Mary Alice sniffed. "He can barely *walk*. What do you think I've been doing all week? I've been giving him ballroom dancing lessons. And the big clodhopper tramped all over my feet. I'm crippled for life."

The route of the parade crossed the Wabash tracks at the depot, to give the other side of town a look. But the Blue Bird train pulled in from Chicago, right on schedule. It blocked the way and separated the parade just ahead of the Weidenbach float, which drew up short.

The Cowgills' overworked old horse dragging our hayframe didn't notice. It clopped on and ran into Mrs.

Weidenbach's float. We bumped. I reached for Mary Alice to keep her from tangling in her skirts and pitching off the float. Mrs. Wilcox teetered on her stool.

Of course Mrs. Weidenbach knew we were right behind her, crabbing her act with an older settler than her daddy. And her reciting nephew had finished out of the money at the talent show, so she was already upset and off her feed with us.

But now her old daddy turned around and looked back. He may not have known where he was, but there was nothing wrong with his eyesight. He read our sign over Uncle Grady, and his old pink eyes narrowed. He spoke sharply to his daughter, who laid a restraining hand on him.

Then it all happened quick. Mrs. Weidenbach's daddy slipped free of her, leaped out of his kitchen chair, and jumped off their float. He cocked his forage cap at a dangerous angle and stalked back to our hayframe.

Glaring up at Uncle Grady, he howled, "You yellow-bellied old buzzard, if you'd fought in the Mexican War, we'd have lost!"

Seeming to consider this, Uncle Grady gazed down. Then he hollered, "Them's fighting words, and I declare war!" Before Grandma could stop him, he charged off his throne, balanced a moment on the edge of our float, and threw himself into space. He lit on Mrs. Weidenbach's daddy, and they both rolled in the street, locked in combat. Their medals and weaponry clanged like wild bells ringing out.

"Don't use the sword, Uncle Grady!" Grandma cried.

By now the Wabash Blue Bird should have pulled out. But all the passengers were at the windows, staring at this spectacle. Two of the oldest men alive were brawling in the street, tangled up in each other and Uncle Grady's sword, their small fists throwing punches. Now they were so covered in dust and droppings, you couldn't tell one uniform from the other. In the distance from the other side of town the last of the high-school bands blared "The Stars and Stripes Forever."

At length Mrs. Weidenbach separated the two old warriors, though her hoopskirt got in the way. Grandma would have let them fight it out.

She came to the depot to see us off on the day we left. It was to be our last visit together, and I suppose she knew. But she didn't say so.

As the Blue Bird appeared down the tracks, I had something to ask her. "Grandma, there's a loose end in my mind."

"Well, don't trip over it," she said.

"How do you know Uncle Grady Griswold is a hundred and three years old?"

"How do you know he's not?" She held her spidery old black umbrella between herself and the sun.

"What I mean is, does he have a birth certificate or something like that?"

"A birth certificate?" She waved me away. "They didn't have birth certificates in them days. You were just born, and people accepted it."

But now the train was pulling in, hissing steam, so

that was her last word. As Mary Alice and I scrambled aboard, Grandma heaved up a picnic hamper for us.

We were hardly out of town before we were both slumped half-asleep in the seat. A trip to Grandma really took it out of you. Dozing, I heard a mew. I looked down at our feet to see the lid rising on the picnic hamper. Two green eyes peered out.

I shot a look at Mary Alice, who was only pretending to be asleep. "What's that?"

She blinked in surprise at the green eyes blinking back. "For heaven's sake," she said. "It's the kitten. Poor little thing. It took her three days to find her way back from Uncle Grady's to the cobhouse. Grandma must have stuck her in the hamper, meaning me to have her. What a surprise."

"And yet you don't look too surprised."

"You could knock me over with a feather." Mary Alice sniffed, and lifted the kitten onto her lap.

"How do you know Mother's going to let you keep that kitten?"

"How do you know she's not?" said Mary Alice.

And we steamed on, riding the Wabash Blue Bird, bound for Chicago across the patchwork fields.

The Troop Train

———∞∞∞———

1942

The years went by, and Mary Alice and I grew up, slower than we wanted to, faster than we realized. Another war came, World War II, and I wanted to get in it. The war looked like my chance to realize my old dream of flying. My soul began to swoop as it had all those years ago at the county fair when I'd had my first ride in Barnie Buchanan's biplane. I only hoped the war would last long enough to make a flier out of me, and so it did.

I joined up at Fort Sheridan for the Army Air Corps. But before I could go to flight school, I had to do basic training down at Camp Leonard Wood.

On the night we were shipping out from Dearborn Station, it occurred to me that the troop train would pass through Grandma's town, sometime in the night. I sent her a telegram. She never did have a phone. A telegram might give her a turn, but I just wanted to tell her the train would be going through town, though it wouldn't stop.

In the way of troop trains, we left an hour late and sat on the siding outside Joliet for another hour. You don't get any sleep on a troop train. Our car was blue with smoke and noisy with a floating crap game. I sat through the long night, propped at the window.

Then I knew we were getting to Grandma's town. It was sound asleep in the hour before dawn. We slowed past the depot, and now we were coming to Grandma's, the last house in town. It was lit up like a jack-o'-lantern. Every window upstairs and down blazed, though she always turned out the light when she left a room. Now we were rolling past, and there was Grandma herself.

She stood at her door, large as life—larger, framed against the light from her front room. Grandma was there, watching through the watches of the night for the train to pass through. She couldn't know what car I was in, but her hand was up, and she was waving—waving big at all the cars, hoping I'd see.

And I waved back. I waved long after the window filled with darkness and long distance.